Wait for Me, Watch for Me, Eula Bee

Lewallen saw Many Horses' pony fall, rump over head, throwing the Comanche to the ground, its front hoof caught in a prairie-dog hole.

Many Horses bounded to his feet to face the herd and stood for a long moment as the panic stricken buffalo came running at him, parting to his left and right, to avoid colliding with Lewallen's pony. Lewallen saw the flash of the chief's eyes, seeking his, as the dun pony raced toward him, and he saw the Indian's hand outstretched toward him.

Without thinking of his own safety or of anything but the hundreds of buffalo thundering behind him, Lewallen reached his left hand out and down to Many Horses. . . .

BY PATRICIA BEATTY

Wait for Me, Watch for Me, Eula Bee

PATRICIA BEATTY

 A BEECH TREE PAPERBACK BOOK NEW YORK

The Library of Congress has cataloged the Morrow Junior Books
edition of *Wait for Me, Watch for Me, Eula Bee* as follows:

Beatty, Patricia.
Wait for me, watch for me, Eula Bee
    Summary: With his father and brother serving in the
Confederate Army and the rest of his family murdered in a
Comanche raid of their west Texas farm, 13-year-old Lewallen
seeks to free himself and his younger sister from their Indian
captivity. ISBN 0-688-22151-3 — ISBN 0-688-32151-8 lib. bdg.
  [1. Indians of North America—Captivity—Fiction.
  2. Comanche Indians—Fiction. 3. The West—Fiction.] I. Title.
PZ7.B380544 Wai [Fic] 78-12782

10 9 8 7 6 5 4 3 2
First Beech Tree Edition, 1990
ISBN 0-688-10077-5

For Carl

Contents

Wait for Me, Watch for Me, Eula Bee

ONE

"Maybe They Won't Come"

Leaning against a porch post of the cabin, Lewallen Collier looked on unhappily as his father, Joe, and his oldest brother, Johnny, mounted up to ride away to join the Confederate Army. Their saddlebags were bulging with food. Bedrolls and canteens were tied to the back of their saddles, and each man was armed with a Bowie knife and a pistol. The older Collier rode with a musket across the front of his saddle within easy reach of his hand. Who knew what dangers they might run into on their long journey to Houston? Wild animals, outlaws, Indians—or maybe now that the War had come—Yankees not yet driven out of Texas.

Although Joe and Johnny Collier went out well armed, Lewallen knew they had left weapons behind—a pistol for himself and Daniel, his younger brother, a rifle for his mother, Elizabeth, and another for her old uncle Joshua, not to mention the pitchforks and hoes that could be used as weapons in time of danger.

The farewells were brief and strained. Joe Collier had a hug for each child and a kiss for his wife. She didn't want him to go off to war so soon and had asked him in vain not to volunteer and to wait to be called up. He didn't speak to her now, but to her uncle said, "You look after them, Josh. I say Johnny and me'll be back here farming a year from this time, in the spring or the summer of sixty-two at the latest. It won't take long for us Texas sharpshooters to whip them Yankees to a standstill and get the Civil War over and done with." Then as Uncle Joshua had nodded, agreeing with him, Joe Collier's gaze had gone searchingly from Lewallen's face to Daniel's, in turn, and he had said to them, "You boys, promise me to obey your ma and Uncle Josh and watch out for your little sister, Eula Bee. See that she don't get into any mischief. Keep her away from those no-good neighbors of ours, them Cabrals."

"Yes, Pa," was all Lewallen said, though he felt like shouting, You don't have to volunteer so soon. You can wait, Pa! You can wait, Johnny!

Johnny, who was all too eager to go off to win the War, called out from atop his frisky sorrel, "I'll bring a Yankee soldier's hat back for each of you boys and for you, Ma, a fringed, silk shawl and a real-true China doll for Eula Bee."

Thirteen-year-old Lewallen noticed that his words brought only a wan smile from Mrs. Collier but a joyous one from his three-year-old, redheaded sister, Eula Bee, who was too young to understand anything but the promise of getting a present from her beloved Johnny. He understood, though, and so did his mother. He and his mother were alike, not redheaded, freckly, and brown-eyed like the rest of the family but thin, dark-haired, and gray-eyed. He and she thought alike, too. They knew that they were being left to defend their land—a frail woman, an old man, and two half-grown boys, himself and Daniel.

Going to stand beside his mother as his father and Johnny rode off out of sight beyond the post oaks that bordered the road to the creek, Lewallen was the only one to hear her murmur, "May God watch over us all."

Uncle Joshua, who was too far away to hear, turned to Daniel. "You got the loudest whistle here, Dan'l. Run down to the creek and whistle that fool of a dog Rascal back here where he belongs. Don't let him follow your pa and Johnny off to Houston. The Confederate Army don't need that bag of fleas. Then you come right back here. You and me and Lewtie haven't got the morning chores done yet, remember. Just because some of the Colliers ride off to war don't mean that the world's come to an ending and the green things are going to stop growing."

Lewallen watched his mother take Eula Bee sadly by the hand and lead her into the kitchen end of the double cabin. Uncle Joshua watched her, then said, "Lewtie, your ma, even as a girl, was ever inclined to look on the dark side of things."

"Uncle Josh, Ma didn't want to come all the way out to West Texas where it's so lonesome. East Texas would've suited her better."

"Now, Lewtie, what difference does it make? Your pa would've gone off to war from there, too."

The boy stood with folded arms and said solemnly, "Uncle Josh, there are a lot more folks in East Texas. It'd be safer there. There are panthers and wolves and bad neighbors hereabouts, like them Cabrals, and there are Indians, too. There are so many kinds of Indians that you don't always know who's friendly and who ain't."

"Truly said, Lewtie. That's why all of us got to stay in

sight of the cabin and keep a musket or pistol close to hand."

Lewallen went into the sleeping part of the double log house and took down a heavy loaded pistol, from where it hung on the wall, and put it into his belt. Bending over to weed would be even harder work with the pistol on, but from now on it would be with him all the time, even under his pillow at night. His pa had taught him to fire it with some accuracy, but he hoped he wouldn't need to, unless it was at a thieving chicken hawk. He sighed, thinking of his pa's farewell words.

"Watch out for Eula Bee. Keep her away from them Cabrals." He meant don't let her mix with their little gal, Angelita, and the same thing ought to go for Daniel and the Cabral boy, Tomás.

That night Lewallen spoke to his younger brother and got his promise to stay clear of Tomás Cabral; afterward he spoke to Eula Bee about Angelita. She nodded wisely at him with her finger in her mouth as if she understood what he was saying. If she didn't, Lewallen would teach her by refusing to sing her favorite song, "Lorena," for a while. How she doted on that tune, following him around, begging him over and over to sing or whistle it for her.

He told her straight out in Daniel's and his ma's hearing, "Eula Bee, if you slip out to see Angelita Cabral, I'm gonna refuse to sing "Lorena" every time you ask me. Do you promise me that you won't go out of sight of Ma and the house?"

"I promise, Lewtie," had been her response, and everyone had smiled.

*   *   *

Yet three days later, when Lewallen came in from the hot work of weeding the cornfield to get another bucket of drinking water for him and Daniel, he found Eula Bee gone from the house. His mother asked him, "Is your sister with you boys out in the field?"

"No. Maybe she's with Uncle Josh. Where is he?"

His mother went on churning butter outside the cabin as she said, "In the barn. I suspect she's with him."

Lewallen set his bucket down and went quickly to the barn where he found the old man milking. "Is Eula Bee here with you, Uncle Josh?"

"Nope." The old man looked at him out of bleary eyes. "Last I saw of her she was heading your way to the cornfield, her and Rascal."

Swiftly Lewallen searched the corral, pigsty, privy, smokehouse, and springhouse. She wasn't at any of them. Going behind the house at a walk so as not to alarm his mother, he started to run as he headed for the creek, the forbidden place. Halfway there, in the unplanted field the Colliers might put to corn next spring, he whistled for Rascal and was rewarded by barking. Running faster and becoming drenched with sweat, Lewallen came pell-mell through the cottonwoods to the creek bank, looking up and down.

"Eula Bee?" he shouted at the top of his lungs.

There was no answer from her, but Rascal, their blue-tick hound, came bounding and barking toward him out of a clump of brush not far from the water. Lewallen made for it at once, pulled the stalks apart, and discovered his sister crouching beneath them. She was head to head with Angelita Cabral, playing with cornhusk dolls, just as she promised not to. Both little girls started to wail at the sight of his anger-flushed face looming above them.

He bellowed at the black-haired Mexican child, "You get on home!" Reaching down, he grabbed her by the shoulders and jerked her to her feet.

Lewallen was about to set her, howling shrilly, onto the first stepping stone in the creek when he heard a deep voice shouting fiercely. "You stop that, boy. You hurt my gal, and I'll put a bullet through your leg."

It was old man Cabral himself, standing on the other side of the water. He had a big pistol trained on Lewallen. "Let go of her, and don't you even think of moving your hand toward your weapon."

"All right." Lewallen took his hands from the girl's shoulders and lifted them into the air.

"Angelita. *Venca. Pronto.*"

Lewallen watched Angelita cross over the stepping stones to her pa's side, where she grabbed him, holding on to one of his long legs, blubbering. He could tell from the small whimpering noises he heard behind him and the sound of brush snapping that Eula Bee was heading for home.

As Lewallen saw the black-browed man put his pistol into his belt, he cried out to him, "Us Colliers don't want to have anything to do with you folks!"

Cabral pried his daughter loose and lifted her up against his shoulder. Then the Mexican called out over the creek, "That suits me and mine just fine and dandy, boy. We don't want any dealings with you no-good gringos either!" He turned his back on Lewallen and strode off through the cottonwoods, where his big black horse waited for him.

Lewallen struck off for home feeling very pleased with himself. But that Eula Bee! She would get a good switching for disobeying. As for old man Cabral, he sure knew where matters stood. Uncle Josh and his mother would say he'd done and said the right things.

The Cabrals were the nearest neighbors the Colliers had, but not the closest by any means. Lewallen's pa had talked to Cabral only once, when the Cabrals had first showed up to settle. He had taken a dislike to Cabral right off because he was so danged unfriendly. He was unfriendly to everybody. It turned out later that nobody around Palo Duro knew anything about the Cabrals except that Mrs. Cabral was Mexican and there were two kids, a boy and a girl. Daniel had made friends with Tomás Cabral, and he claimed Tomás spoke some English. The Cabrals never showed up at barn raisings or camp meetings, and they seldom rode into Palo Duro.

Lewallen had never been close enough to Cabral to see if Pa had been right that the man had green eyes instead of brown ones. But certainly he had been right that Cabral could talk good-enough English.

But that was all the Colliers knew about the Cabrals—that and the rumor that they'd come north from El Paso. Nobody knew whether Cabral had fought in the Mexican war some twenty years back or what side he favored in the Civil War.

Yet Cabral wasn't a person to mess with, even if the sight of him out riding over their land on his red-eyed, black gelding rankled all the Colliers. He most likely wouldn't be any comfort at all to neighbors in time of trouble the way most Texas folks were. Cabral acted as if he was hiding something, according to what Ma said. And Ma was good at sensing things. Yes, sir, old Cabral was truly somebody to watch out for.

Putting Cabral out of his mind as he walked home, Lewallen focused on Eula Bee. Ma would switch her, but he had to punish her, too. He had to live up to what he'd threatened her with if she hung around Angelita Cabral again. He wouldn't sing "Lorena" for a whole month, no matter how hard she begged or wheedled.

Because he knew Eula Bee was out of earshot and he liked the song, too, he began to sing it to himself as he crossed the field that lay below the house.

> The years creep slowly by, Lorena,
> The snow is on the grass again. . . .

Some days after Lewallen's meeting with Cabral three riders came to the Collier farm, first warning of their arrival by shooting a rifle twice into the air. All the same the entire Collier family ran into the house from the fields and barn and greeted the visitors with rifles and pistols from behind the little glassless windows on two sides of the house.

"Hold your fire!" shouted one of the riders, a black-bearded man riding a bay horse.

"Do you know him, Ma? Is he a Yankee, maybe?" Lewallen asked his mother, who stood at the window with him, sighting along her rifle with trembling hands.

"No, I don't, Lewtie, but don't shoot at him yet."

"Yes, Ma."

The two of them waited, and then Uncle Joshua called out from the other side of the house, "He's all right, Elizabeth. I know him. It's Evans from Palo Duro. Let's go out and find out what they want. You, Lewtie, keep tight hold of Rascal's collar, so he don't run at their horses."

As Lewallen struggled with the excited dog, Evans did most of the talking. "I come here to tell you that some of the settlers hereabouts are forting up at one or two places where they'll be safer."

"Forting up?" asked Daniel.

Mrs. Collier turned to speak to him. "It means that we'd be leaving here and going someplace where there's a fort or stockade to protect us." She looked back at Evans. "You want us to come to Palo Duro, I reckon. Who's holding it?"

"Some Texas troops, mostly lame men like me or old ones. But it ain't just Palo Duro, ma'am. Some of the bigger farmhouses are building log stockades. They'd welcome you and your kin."

"I expect they would." Lewallen saw how the corners of his mother's mouth tightened. Then she asked slowly in an unfamiliar voice, one that was cold and grating, "Mister, do the Indians in this part of the state know about the War yet?"

Evans nodded heavily. "We reckon that they do, ma'am. They take notice of things, and sometimes they ride into Palo Duro to trade for tobacco at the general store."

Another rider called out to her, "Ma'am, will you be going to a safer place then?"

"We'll be thinking on it," replied Lewallen's mother.

"And thank you for coming to us with the warning."

Daniel turned about and pointed in the direction of the creek. "Did you go see Mister Cabral, too?"

As Evans shook his head, one of the other riders said angrily, "We signaled to him, and then we rode partway to his cabin. Before we got there, he took a rifle shot at us that was so close it kicked up dust at my horse's front hoof. So we didn't press on to his place."

Old Joshua spoke Lewallen's thought. "Us folks don't have any dealings with Cabral or his family."

Evans grunted. Then, as he swung his horse about to leave, he called over his shoulder, "Well, Josh, if you find a way, tell Cabral that him and his kin are welcome to fort up, too."

Lewallen cried out, laughing, "We'll be sure to tell him for you, mister!"

His mother grabbed him hard by the shoulder. "Lewtie, there ain't one single thing to laugh about that I can see."

Daniel asked her, "Ma, are we going to fort up?"

Uncle Joshua answered, "No, sir. We ain't gonna come back here someday, when we think it's safe again, and find somebody else squatting on our land, saying it's theirs now."

Lewallen's mother spoke wistfully. "No Collier ever gave any trouble to Indians hereabouts that I know of. So maybe we won't be pestered. Maybe they won't come."

"More than likely not, Elizabeth," agreed her uncle. "Now, boys, you get back to work in the garden, but keep in sight of the cabin all the time."

With their pistols in their belts, Lewallen and Daniel

went back to hoeing weeds in the yam hills at one side of the barn.

Daniel spoke first. "Lewtie, Tomás Cabral told me quite awhile back that his pa knows a lot about Indians."

"That don't surprise me much." Lewallen stole a glance at his brother's troubled face. "Maybe Cabral's dealings with the Indians haven't been so peaceable as ours. Did Tomás say that the Indians favored his pa or not?"

Daniel shook his auburn head. "I don't know whether they do or don't. All I know is that Mister Cabral is supposed to know a thing or two about Indians, and Tomás says his pa says Indians are a mighty tricky bunch."

"Maybe he's right, Daniel, but it's hard to tell about anything a Cabral says. Now you be sure to keep away from Tomás like you have been doing."

The month of June 1861 was especially hot and dry. One afternoon Lewallen found himself cussing the weather that made him drip sweat as he carried water to his mother's vegetable garden behind the cabin. Lugging the heavy buckets made his back ache. When he'd emptied the last one, he straightened up with a groan that he'd been saving up till the work was over.

Halfway through that satisfying groan he got the first warning that something was wrong. It came from Rascal, who dashed past him from around the front of the cabin toward a little stand of post oaks a hundred feet from where Lewallen stood. The dog was barking wildly, and the hair on his hackles rose as he plunged into the trees.

An instant later came an agonized howling that made

Lewallen grab for the pistol in his belt. He thought at first it was a coyote lurking in the trees waiting to carry off a hen or one of the piglets. But it couldn't be. A coyote wouldn't attack a good-sized dog. It had to be something big and powerful like a panther.

"Uncle Josh, it's a panther in the oaks!" Lewallen shouted, as he ran forward with his pistol drawn, ready to help Rascal. He knew the old man would hear him and come running, too. He'd been outside sharpening a sickle at the whetstone just a few minutes ago not far away. "Uncle Josh!" shouted the boy once more, trying to hurry him and at the same time scare the panther off with his cries.

All at once Lewallen's shouts were drowned out by a terrible screeching. He knew instantly that this noise didn't come from the throat of any big cat. It was a human sound.

He stopped in his tracks, frozen with shock, as five men on ponies came riding toward him out of the oaks. Their faces were horrible to look at, painted black, and their half-naked bodies gleamed a copper color. Indians! Indians armed with clubs and hatchets.

His trance broken and his heart hammering with fright, Lewallen reacted automatically. He lifted his pistol, aimed at a rider pounding down on him, and pulled the trigger. The hasty shot meant for the Indian's heart wasn't a true one. It struck him in the shoulder, and, at its impact, he fell from his pony.

A second Indian, the one just behind the brave Lewallen had shot, was upon the boy now. Lewallen fired again, but this time the bullet sped over the head of the young warrior. He had two black crow feathers in his hair and was lying along his pony's spine to make himself as small a target as possible. Shrieking like a devil, the brave raced by Lewallen and, as he did, reached out with one hand and gave him a hard slap on the side of the head. *"A-he!"* the Indian yelled, as he sped past.

The warrior galloping behind him did the exact same thing—slapped Lewallen and rode by—but the shoulder of the Indian's pony struck him, knocking him off balance so he swayed trying to keep on his feet.

The fourth rider carried a wooden club. He didn't touch Lewallen with his hand but struck him on his head with the club a second before Lewallen's third bullet creased the brave's scalp. Blood poured down the top of his head and over the black paint.

That welling red stream was the last thing Lewallen saw before he fell, stunned by the blow, face downward onto the sun-baked dirt beside the vegetable garden.

Lewallen couldn't hear the wild screams of his mother or the hoarse shouting of his great-uncle as the war party that had come down on him, attacking the cabin from its rear, joined forces with other raiders attacking from the front. He didn't see Uncle Joshua shoot an Indian off his pony and then be killed himself by three arrows from the young brave with the black feathers. He didn't see this brave and another burst into the kitchen of the cabin and knock the rifle out of his mother's trembling hand and club her to death before she could squeeze off a shot. Lewallen didn't see his panic-stricken brother Daniel killed by a lance as he stood between two rows of tall corn, courageously firing all of his bullets at the riders and hitting none of them.

Still unconscious, Lewallen didn't see his sister hauled, yelling and screaming, out from under his parents' bed, where she'd hidden herself after she'd witnessed Uncle Joshua's killing. Eula Bee was dragged out of the house by one leg, down the porch steps and onto the ground in front of the cabin, where she lay sobbing and wailing, "Mama, Mama." Then after a while she cried more softly, "Johnny, Lewtie!"

He couldn't see the Indians gather together to make a ring around her as she wept and two of them reach out to touch her short, red curls.

TWO
Tomás

Rough hands awakened Lewallen Collier as they flipped him over onto his back so that the sun beat down on his face. He felt a jabbing in his left side as his pistol was jerked out from beneath him. He lay dazed for a moment, surrounded by Indians bending over him. Then all at once he smelled scorching wood and heard a roaring sound of flames, which was mixed with a soft sobbing wail.

The first thing he saw when he opened his eyes was a brown hand holding a blood-smeared knife a few inches from his face. The next moment the same Indian's other hand grabbed his hair and pulled it tight against his scalp. Lewallen was instantly jerked to a sitting posture.

Too shocked by the suddenness to cry out, he stared up into the painted, sweat-streaked face of a young Indian who was about to stab and scalp him. Before the knife could descend to his chest, though, the scalper's wrist was grabbed by an older brave, who shouted some words that made the first Indian glare at him. But at the same time he let go of Lewallen's hair and straightened up. All at once Lewallen recognized the warrior who meant to scalp him as the second attacking Indian, the one with the crow feathers, who hit him and then galloped past. The older brave was someone Lewallen had not seen before. Like the others, he was dressed in beaded moccasins, ornamented breechcloth, and buckskin leggings, but unlike them he wore a bonnet of buffalo fur decorated with feathers. The lance in his left hand was trimmed with eagle feathers. This older warrior gazed at Lewallen out of flat, dark eyes, then made a commanding gesture to two other Indians and walked away with the younger warrior. The braves he'd made the gesture to prodded the boy in the rump with their feet, and when he didn't get up fast enough to suit them, they caught him under the arms and hauled him to his feet.

He stood between them, swaying with giddiness as he put one hand to the left side of his head where he'd caught the blow of the war club. There was a swelling, and his hand was sticky with drying blood. Lewallen shook his head to clear it, and, as he did, he saw the rear of the Collier cabin.

It was afire. Flames shot high in the air while around it swarmed a number of Indians. Some were trying to catch the Collier chickens that were fleeing in all directions. Others were perched on the railing of the pigsty shooting arrows into the squealing pigs. The two plow horses were running loose, and the one saddle horse Pa had left at home had a rope about her neck and was tied to one of the nearby post oaks. The corpses of their mules lay stretched out beside the barn, where they'd been killed with lances as they ran. Near the mare stood a group of little ponies with stirrupless saddles and Indian-style bridles that fit over their lower teeth. Lewallen looked on as a raider came walking toward him from around the front of the house. He was laughing and carrying a squirming, kicking, wailing burden under one arm—Eula Bee—and a sack of sugar under the other.

"Eula Bee!" shouted Lewallen.

She lifted her head, stared at him, and then started to scream at the top of her lungs.

"Eula Bee." He started forward, but his two Indian guards caught him by the arms, stopping him. One of them said something sharply to him in his own language. Lewallen guessed it meant not to move. He obeyed.

He looked on in an agony as he saw his sister brought to a spot under a tree and dropped down where a brave with a shoulder wound sat propped up against the trunk. Now Lewallen remembered. He was the Indian he'd shot—the first one to attack him. He sure wasn't dying, though. The brave held a knife in his hand, and, as the boy watched, he made a fierce face and brandished the knife before the terrified little girl, who hid her face in her arms.

"Eula Bee!" Lewallen shouted once more.

"Lewtie, Lewtie!" she cried out, lifting her head. She would have run to him but was caught by the collar and hauled back by the wounded Indian.

"*Kima!*" One of the men holding Lewallen ordered, taking him away from his sister.

Horror took hold of Lewallen as he rounded the corner of the cabin and saw the body of his great-uncle lying with his head in a pool of blood not ten feet from the whetstone. There was no sign of his mother, but the kitchen end of the cabin was ablaze and he sensed that she, too, was dead. If Uncle Josh had died where he was, Lewallen was certain that she wouldn't have gotten away. He'd heard the old man's voice calling to his mother just before the war party had attacked, and at the time his mother had been busy in the kitchen. Daniel? Lewallen checked an impulse to shout his brother's name and hope for an answer. Where was he? He'd been out in the cornfield, away from the house and yard. Had he gotten away and hidden? He dared not call his name and alert the Indians. Lewallen's lips began to move in prayer for his brother as he stared at the blazing house his father and Uncle Josh had built with so much effort.

He watched as two warriors ran to the burning house with pieces of wood, held them to the flames till they caught fire, and then ran toward the barn and the other smaller farm buildings to set them ablaze. He looked on helplessly as more Indians joined the party that had attacked the Colliers. They drove steers ahead of them, cattle Lewallen recognized as his father's entire meager stock. One of the Indians who had set fire to the barn led the milk cow out to the steers. The Indian leader who had saved his life stepped forward to inspect the cattle, nodded, stepped back, raised his lance, and called out some words. One of Lewallen's guards shouted, grabbing his hair and twisting it hard.

But the Indian wearing the buffalo-fur bonnet cried out at Lewallen's captor, leveled his lance at the guards, and called out a longer string of words. Afterward Lewallen's hands were tied behind him with a leather rope.

At another shout from their leader all of the dismounted Indians started toward their ponies carrying what they'd plundered—an iron kettle, struggling chickens, quilts from the beds, a wide-brimmed, leather hat of Uncle Joshua's, and all of the firearms the Colliers owned. As Lewallen stood between his guards, he saw his great-uncle's rifle in the hands of one brave and his pistol in the belt of the leader. Another brave carried the rifle his mother had kept in the kitchen, which confirmed to Lewallen that she was dead.

He fought back tears for his mother and Uncle Josh but also for Eula Bee, Daniel, and himself. He must keep his mind on the three of them, he told himself.

Suddenly a wave of sick horror swept over him. If one of the guards hadn't held him up, he would have collapsed. Lewallen recognized Daniel's pistol in the belt of the young warrior who had been going to scalp him. It was his brother's, all right. Lewallen knew it by its carved elkhorn handle, the painstaking handiwork of his great-uncle.

Silently Lewallen recited the Lord's Prayer as a farewell to his mother, brother, and Uncle Joshua.

He was still saying it, stumbling over the words, when he was propelled to the stand of trees where his guards' ponies waited for them. The buffalo-fur-bonnet leader had mounted a pinto and had ridden to one side to supervise the mounting of the others, who secured their plunder to their ponies however they could. He motioned toward Lewallen and then to the Collier mare, and his guards lifted him onto the saddleless buckskin horse, which they led behind them with the leather rope about her neck.

Lewallen looked frantically about him. Eula Bee? Where was she? Had she been murdered, too, while he'd been taken around to the front of the cabin?

No, thank God, there she was, sitting on a pony in front

of an Indian, who held her tightly across the chest. She was weeping.

"Eula Bee!" Lewallen shouted to her.

"Lewtie," she answered softly.

Beyond Eula Bee and her captor was the wounded Indian, on a pony, too. Two other braves rode beside him, ready to help him should he fall.

Lewallen counted. One, two, three—twenty-one Indians. He didn't know their tribe or why they'd attack his family, but there were twenty-one of them in the war party.

They should have forted up in Palo Duro. His pa should never have come to West Texas in the first place, knowing that the War was on its way and that he'd be going off to fight in it before too long. Uncle Josh and his pa should have listened to his mother.

"Lewtie, Lewtie," rose Eula Bee's cry.

Because he couldn't do anything else to comfort her, and in spite of his dry throat and aching head, Lewallen began to sing the tune she loved so much.

> *The sun's low down the sky, Lorena.*
> *A frost gleams where the flowers have been. . . .*

As he rode among the Indians away from the blazing pyre that had been the Collier farm he shut his eyes tight and sang the same words over and over. He couldn't remember the other lines of the song. Lewallen wasn't aware of the many curious glances that came his way from the members of the war party. The Indian leader, who rode at the head of the swiftly moving band of warriors, turned about to look at the Texas boy again and again while his guard, with the crow feathers, glanced angrily at him.

After a time, a feeling of numbness came over Lewallen. His skull pounded drumlike with every step his horse took. It was as if he'd entered another world, one where nothing was real. It was as if he rode among these Indians in a terrible, shimmering dream, singing the same mournful words of "Lorena" over and over again.

Lewallen had no idea of how many miles they'd traveled when the Indians halted at dusk along a creek. The country was strange to him, but he knew that they had ridden west because they rode toward the dying sun of that hideous day.

Two warriors dragged him off the mare and let him fall to the prairie while they squatted near the stream, eating dried food from the bags they carried and drinking from the stream. Raising his aching head with effort, Lewallen peered about in spite of his giddiness, looking for his sister. He saw her being given food and water from a buffalo pouch by the young Indian with the crow feathers who had wanted to kill him.

A wave of fury and nausea swept over Lewallen, and he shouted, "You get away from my sister!"

"Lewtie!" Eula Bee began to struggle and tried to move away from the squatting Indian, but he grabbed her by her skirt and pulled her back, laughing at her futile kicking.

A little later two Indian youths came over to Lewallen, not to untie him or feed him but to give him water. One pried his jaws open, while the other poured water from a gourd. And then once more Lewallen was lifted onto his horse. This time his ankles were tied together under the mare's belly so he could not fall off, although he might be dragged upside down if he didn't keep his seat. His rump ached from the pressure of the mare's spine.

They rode most of the night over the prairie under a full moon. Sometime in the early hours of the morning, just before the moon disappeared, they came to a gap between a long line of low, black hills. He recalled his father saying that he'd heard there were hills to the west and one was said to have a notch through which the buffalo herds passed.

His captors stopped there under the light of the descending moon as if they were waiting for something. At dawn Lewallen found what it was. More Indians came riding over the prairie, nineteen of them this time, driving horses, mules, and cattle with them.

Maybe there had been two war parties. Or, more than likely, one large one had split into two to attack the farms in their part of Texas.

These warriors had captives also. Lewallen drew in his breath in a gasp at what he saw. The second group of raiders yesterday must have gone to the Cabral place. Their captives were Angelita Cabral, who was being held onto a pony by a brave just as Eula Bee was, and Tomás, her ten-year-old brother, tied by his ankles to a horse led by an Indian. Lewallen's gaze swept over the horses the Indians had stolen. He was looking for Cabral's big black, but it wasn't there. Still, the children's parents were surely dead.

Eula Bee, who'd just awakened, had seen the Cabrals, too. She let out a sharp cry, which made Angelita wail in return. Tomás lifted his head and stared about him as the two groups of Indians joined. His eyes met Lewallen's with recognition, and as he passed by with his captor he murmured nine soft words, "Comanches and a Kiowa next to you. Show bravery."

Lewallen cried out after him, "Daniel's dead. So's our ma and Uncle Joshua. Did they kill your folks, too?"

All Lewallen could see was the back of the Mexican boy's head. Tomás nodded; then he shook his head. One was killed, but was the other alive? Could it be that Cabral was still alive?

Lewallen's thoughts sped from Cabral to the Indians. Comanches and Kiowas, who he knew were the allies of the Comanches. The two fiercest of the Plains tribes! Daniel had said that Tomás had told him that his father knew about Indians. He'd better talk to Tomás as soon as he could. After all, Tomás knew what kind of Indians they were.

Cold fright gripped Lewallen as he remembered the tales he'd heard about what happened to Indian captives. He shuddered as he watched little Angelita ride by, held fast by her grim captor, a man with a heavy-jowled face. What would lie ahead for himself, the Cabrals, and Eula Bee? "Show bravery" was what Tomás had advised.

He was the eldest of the four captives, so he should be the bravest to set an example for them. But how brave could he be if he was put to the test? As brave as when the doctor in Palo Duro had pulled out two of his teeth with blacksmith's pliers? He'd yelled then and had shed tears that made Johnny hoot. He'd bellowed like a stuck hog when his pa had poured horse liniment into an ax cut and yelled plenty when his great-uncle sewed it up. No, Lewallen Collier surely wasn't the boldest and bravest thing that ever came over the pike.

As the combined war party started to move again, Lewallen found himself wondering what had delayed the second group. Had Cabral fought them off a long time from his cabin, or had they searched all over his land to round up his cattle and horses? This second group of raiders drove more animals than the first, for Cabral had run more cattle on his land.

A hope rose in his heart as his horse was pulled along beside his fierce Indian guard he knew now was a Kiowa. When they stopped again, Lewallen planned to try hard to talk with Tomás Cabral. He wanted to find out what Tomás had meant by shaking his head and why Tomás's group came up later and by a different route to the rendezvous. But more important was to find out what he had meant by his words of advice.

Though the Indians stopped for a time at another stream to water their ponies and the livestock and eat, Lewallen didn't get a chance to talk with Tomás. The young Kiowa who led his horse and another brave untied the thongs on his ankles and jerked him down off the mare. Together they pushed him down onto the grass in a sitting position. Once again he was given water and this time a piece of salty, rock-hard, sinewy meat that made his head ache even more as he moved his jaws to chew it. As the Indians loosened his feet he saw to his dismay that Tomás was at least fifty feet away, closer to Eula Bee than to him. Angelita was nearest, weeping and digging her small fists into her eyes. She was so little and so wretched. He wished he could call out to her in her own language to comfort her. The best thing he could do, though, for any of them was to stay quiet.

A group of braves were standing around Eula Bee, passing her rigid, little body from man to man, touching her red
hair and soft, freckled cheeks while she stared up in fear.
If she began to wail, God only knew what they might do to
her. Lewallen was greatly relieved when he saw the Indian
leader carrying her off to his pony. She was to ride with
him now, it seemed, and he was the warrior who had
stopped the Kiowa from killing Lewallen. Perhaps he meant
to protect Eula Bee, too.

Tied back on his mare again, Lewallen found himself
with a different Indian companion this time. As they rode
together he eyed Lewallen now and then but not with the
anger that the boy had sensed in the Kiowa. He seemed
only a burden to the new brave, who must see that he did
not escape.

The young Kiowa had gone ahead to ride two ponies
behind the leader. He didn't look back from his new position in the long line of warriors when Lewallen started to
whistle "Lorena" to comfort Eula Bee. The Indian beside
him sucked in his breath, however, and most of the others
turned their heads to stare at the whistling boy.

THREE

"Show Bravery"

Sometime during the hot afternoon the Indians halted and gave the captives more dried meat and water. To Lewallen's joy, Tomás was taken from his horse and thrown down on the prairie not far from him. During an interval while the Indians were leading their ponies away to be watered at a small lake, Lewallen felt it would be safe to call out to Tomás.

"What're they going to do with us, Tom Cabral?"

"Make slaves of us—if we are lucky," was the soft reply.

"Slaves!" The word seared into Lewallen's brain. He'd seen black slaves owned by white men in Palo Duro. Would he and Eula Bee be slaves of Indians? It was unthinkable. Things like that couldn't happen.

Tomás cried out, "I do not know if my father was killed. They were shooting at him with their arrows."

Lewallen only nodded impatiently. Cabral's fate seemed of little importance to him at this moment. He asked anxiously, "Where are they taking us?"

"To their camp." Tomás would have said more, but at that instant the young Kiowa walked by and gave him a kick in the hip. Lewallen noticed once more that this brave wasn't like the thickset Comanches; he was taller and slimmer, and his face, though painted black, was done in a different manner. His hair, however, was the most unusual thing about him and very different from that of the Comanches. It was plaited in three braids on the left side of his head; one braid was so long that it nearly reached to the top of his moccasins. The other side of his hair was chopped off very short, unlike the breast-length, pig-tailed hair of the Comanches. The Kiowa's braids gleamed in the sun, and the two crow feathers stuck in his hair fluttered in the prairie breezes as he stood over Tomás.

Lewallen watched the young Indian narrowly, wondering what he meant to do to Tomás and wondering even more what he was saying. Whatever it was, it made the Comanche who wore the buffalo-fur war bonnet turn away from lifting one of his pony's hooves, look sharply at him, and bark, "*Keta! To-hima!*"

Lewallen guessed from his tone that *keta* meant "don't," and when he saw Tomás lifted by the scowling young Kiowa and put onto the horse he'd been riding, he knew the meaning of the command "*to-hima*" also. By the sudden look of surprise on Tomás's face Lewallen learned that he didn't know the Comanche language. What was more, Lewallen sensed that although the Kiowa traveled and raided with these Comanches, the feeling between him and the leader of the war party wasn't good. Was it because the Comanche had stopped the Kiowa from scalping him?

He was still wondering when, aching from riding bareback for hours, he was lifted by two braves and put onto his mare once more. Now there was more misery to consider as he rode northwest with the raiders.

Eula Bee was sitting on the Kiowa's pony as the war party left the little prairie lake. The Indian was speaking softly to her, dangling the necklace of pipestone he'd taken off. Now and then he touched her red hair, causing fear and hatred to surge up in Lewallen each time.

He wasn't able to speak to Tomás Cabral again the rest of that day. When they camped that night among cotton-woods beside a broad, red-water stream, the captives were kept apart from each other and surrounded by Indians. Lewallen, after he'd been fed, was permitted to walk beside the stream with a Comanche guard. By standing on tiptoe and craning his head, he was able to catch a glimpse of his sister, who'd fallen asleep on a blanket spread out on the ground. Tomás was seated, eating, and Angelita was sleeping a distance away.

That night, in spite of his aching head and his fear and anxiety about the future, Lewallen slept, too. He slept on the hard, windswept ground, while the Indians passed a pipe from hand to hand as they sat by a small campfire.

Riding off in the morning, Lewallen felt better. His head was clearer and his body refreshed, but in his heart he felt greater worry than ever because he sensed they would soon arrive at the Comanche camp. The Indians seemed gay, laughing and calling to each other, and less on their guard.

Although his thoughts were often of his mother and Daniel, he was afraid to let his tears fall, especially since the Indians seemed to be looking at him so often. Tomás had said, "Show bravery," which certainly meant no weeping.

Lewallen vowed to set aside mourning for his family until he could grieve unseen. He'd choke on his grief before he'd cry in front of anyone. That's what Pa would want him to do.

Now he had to keep his wits about him and his mind on Eula Bee and himself. So this morning, as they rode beside the Comanche who led his mare, he sang "Lorena" over and over to let his sister know that he was thinking of her. Let the Comanches make what they could of that.

They came the next morning to a place of wooded canyons, very different country from any Lewallen had ever known in Texas. There lay the camp of the Comanches.

The camp was arranged in Comanche fashion along the banks of a curving little river. Individual buffalo-hide lodges were set away from one another, and there were sleeping arbors made of brush near each tepee. The war party, their faces still painted, rode into the camp after one of the youngest Indians had galloped ahead heralding a victory. Women and children came up from the banks of the river, and old men crept out of the tepees to look on as the warriors paraded by. Many of the Indian women cried out the same words again and again to them, words that Lewallen guessed were greetings or the names of the men. Some of the smaller boys, who were dressed only in breechclouts, came running through the ponies up to him and Tomás to touch their legs playfully and shriek *"A-he,"* before darting back out of the reach of the annoyed warriors.

After the war party had passed, many of the onlookers got onto ponies, too, and followed the braves, all the time shouting and calling back and forth in excitement to one another.

By the time the war party had reached the center of the camp, where many lodges stood together in a circle around a red-painted tepee, there were several hundred Indians following behind the raiders, along with many lean, barking dogs. The noise was so painfully loud that it made Lewallen want to press his hands against his injured head and grit his teeth.

The warriors rode to the central lodge and halted before the man standing at the entrance. A middle-aged Comanche, he wore a broad-brimmed, brown-felt settler's hat and was wrapped in a yellow-and-black blanket robe.

The leader of the war party, still wearing his fur bonnet, rode forward, holding his feathered lance high. When he halted, the Indian with the broad-brimmed hat, the peace chief, raised his hand. Silence came down instantly over the camp except for the dogs. Some of them were booted in the ribs and slunk off howling.

While the peace chief greeted the war chief and the war chief gave a long speech in return about the success of the raid, Lewallen looked about him trying to find Eula Bee in the throng. When he spotted his sister, Lewallen kept his eyes fixed on her. He saw her being lifted down off the pony she was riding by a fat old Indian woman. Once she had Eula Bee on the ground, she got Angelita down, too. Taking each child by the hand, the woman hauled them, stumbling with weariness, to a tepee near the red lodge. There she ducked down and pushed them in before her through the black entry hole. Though he was still greatly worried, Lewallen was relieved to see a woman with his sister. She had handled the two girls very gently. Now Lewallen searched out Tomás and found him staring directly at him with a look of tight-lipped misery on his face. He was trying not to weep and inclined his head in a nod that signaled Lewallen to look in that direction.

What he saw made him catch his breath in horror, then clench his fists in a wave of fury. The young Kiowa sat on his pony on the edge of the war party, holding his lance aloft so that all of the Indians could see it clearly. Tied to its point were three ghastly things that fluttered in the light wind. Hair. Scalps! Lewallen knew them by sight. The gray one was Uncle Joshua's, the auburn-red Daniel's, and the long, dark hair rippling down the shaft of the lance his mother's. Lewallen twisted his hands trying to free them, but the leather rope about his wrists was too tight. If he could have gotten loose then, he would have run to the Kiowa's pony, jerked him off it, and with his bare hands choked him.

"No, boy, no!" Lewallen heard a voice hissing softly nearby. He looked across at Tomás again, but it wasn't he.

"Here, down here," came the very soft words. Lewallen glanced down to the right of his horse. A slender woman stood there, looking down at her moccasins. Had she called out to him in *English*? She came closer now, stepping carefully, but with her eyes still down and moving silently. It seemed to him that she did so in order not to be noticed by the Comanches, who were listening spellbound to the words of their war chief. When the woman was at his side, she lifted her head and gave him an intense look out of the bluest eyes he had ever seen. Except for her eyes, however, she was like all the other Indian women. Her braided hair was dark, and her calf-length gown was made of yellow doeskin. Was she a captive, too? he wondered. Whoever she was, she was trying to warn him not to show his grief and anger at the sight of the scalps. She made a swift-waving gesture with one hand, then moved off to stand behind some Comanches. No one had seen her speak to him.

Could he have another friend here in the Indian camp? A feeling of hope surged up in Lewallen that replaced the wild anger he had experienced only moments before.

Terrified, Lewallen spent the remainder of that day tied hand and foot in a Comanche tepee not far from the red lodge. He was tended to by an old woman who fed him boiled venison from a kettle. There was nothing to see but the inside of the dimly lit tepee, which contained only backrests, robes, hides, and a cook fire in the middle. Yet he knew from the noise he heard that the Indians held a great celebration all day long. He could hear their hooting and whooping, the sound of drums, and the thud of many feet. Once during the night three men came to stand over him and talk among themselves. One was the leader of the raiders, the war chief, the second the young Kiowa brave, and the third was the peace chief, who still wore his settler's hat.

Lewallen tried to sit up and say something, but the young Kiowa put his foot onto his chest, pushed him down again, turned about, and went out of the tepee, ducking through the flap. The other two men examined Lewallen by the light of brands taken from the old woman's fire, put them back, and then followed the young brave outside. In his heart Lewallen was sure that the same three had visited Eula Bee and the two Cabrals. Was his sister being treated well by the Indian woman who held her captive?

When he fell at last into a very uneasy sleep, he was still praying that she would be.

The next morning two Comanche braves Lewallen had never seen came to him, cut the bands from his ankles, and jerked him up. His hands still tied, they pushed him out of the lodge. The old woman came after them.

A horde of shrieking women and children greeted Lewallen as he stood blinking in the morning sunlight, swallowing hard with fright, trying to hang on to his courage. One lean dog, bolder than the others, rushed in, yapping, to nip at his ankles. Out of reflex, more than anything else, Lewallen kicked at it without hitting it. But at his action a shout went up from the Indians. They liked what he'd tried to do. Now the men caught hold of him, one on each side, and pushed through the Comanches. Lewallen glanced about him hoping to spy Eula Bee or one of the Cabrals or the blue-eyed woman who had warned him yesterday, but he saw only Indian women and children, staring at him with looks of fierce eagerness on their faces. Their expressions made his heart pound harder against his ribs. Where were the other captives and the other men? he asked himself.

He learned soon enough as his guards approached the red-painted lodge. Before it on a buffalo robe sat the peace chief and with him the war chief. Not far away, lounging on a blanket in front of a group of braves clustered around a pole festooned with scalps, was the young Kiowa.

"*A-he, a-he!*" the Kiowa cried out, as Lewallen and his guards, followed by the crowd of Indian women and children, came to stand before the pole.

"*A-he, a-he!*" came deeply from the throat of another warrior. Lewallen knew him to be the Comanche who had knocked him senseless with the war club during the attack.

Now everyone sent up a wild clamor. While the Indians were still shouting and yelling, Lewallen saw Tomás Cabral being shoved through the crowd from another direction, the women and children surging around, trying to strike or pinch him. Lewallen was swung about by his guards to face Tomás, and at the same time a brave grabbed the front of Lewallen's shirt and ripped it down the front. Tomás's shirt was in tatters from the rough handling he'd received, and, as Lewallen watched, the crowd pushed Tomás to the ground.

Tomás was hauled to his feet by his hair. One of his Comanche captors put a Bowie knife in his hand and pointed to Lewallen while the other warrior still gripped him by his hair.

Lewallen drew in his breath in shock. Did they want Tomás to kill him with the Bowie knife?

Lewallen felt this hands cut free and his right arm being pinched sharply. His hand was pried open, and a knife identical to Tomás's thrust into it. The guard gave Lewallen a hard shove in the back, making him stumble toward Tomás.

Now he understood. They were to fight each other to entertain the camp!

Lewallen stared at Tomás, who stared back at him. He

thought of Daniel, who had called this Mexican boy his friend. Daniel was dead, murdered by these Indians. So was his mother and old Uncle Josh, and now he was to kill Tomás to give the Comanches something exciting to watch. There was no doubt that Lewallen would be the victor in such a fight. He was half a head taller than Tomás and older. It wouldn't be any contest at all.

What could he do? Lewallen looked about him, taking note of the ring of excited Indians, watching him, waiting for him to rush at Tomás. What should he do now? Throw the knife down onto the ground and refuse to pick it up again? If he did, what would the Indians do to him and Tomás afterward? He was sure it would be something dreadful.

While Lewallen hesitated, he heard that sharp cry *"A-he"* once more. It was the sole sound to be heard in the camp except for that of a nickering pony down by the river.

"Ya-h-h-h!" A wild, furious shout burst from Lewallen's throat as he spun around, knife in hand, and plunged at the man who'd cried *"A-he."* He knew the voice was that of the young Kiowa. The cry had told Lewallen what he should do, and he'd acted at once without reflecting on bravery. The violent rage that had been burning in him for days erupted into frenzied action as he plunged toward the Indian who'd wanted to kill him. His ears were deaf to the delighted shouting of the Comanches.

As the Kiowa flung up his arm to ward off Lewallen's leaping attack and gain time to draw his own knife, the young Texan cut along his arm and then slashed along his painted chest in a long slanting motion that didn't cut

deeply but brought forth a torrent of blood. With his un-
cut arm the young warrior fended Lewallen off and then,
rolling onto his back, kicked him in the stomach, making
Lewallen double over even though the kick didn't have
the full strength of the Kiowa's powerful leg in it.

"*A-he, a-he!*" rose delightedly from the crowd, which
seemed wonderfully pleased.

Lewallen felt strong hands grab him and jerk him backward, dragging him, still doubled over from the kick, to
where the two men sat before the red tepee. Two braves
held Lewallen as he struggled and bucked, while a third
pried his hand open to make him drop the knife.

A bellowed command made him straighten up and look
into the eyes of the Comanche peace chief. He looked
searchingly at Lewallen, then said one word only, "*Yee!*"
It sounded like a word of astonishment.

"*Tsaa,*" murmured the Comanche war chief softly.

The peace chief waved his hand, and Lewallen was
propelled by his guards away from the red lodge through
the quiet, staring throng toward a nearby tepee, which
had been painted with a sun and horses on its sides. They
pushed him through the flap opening, down onto a pile
of skins, and left him there unbound.

The sound of a voice greeted him over the singing and
dancing, which had started the moment after he'd entered
the lodge. The words were in English. "Do not be afraid,
boy."

The voice was that of the blue-eyed lady who had
spoken to him before. He sat up, peering into the dimness.
He could see someone sitting on the far side of the tepee
across from him. "Who are you, ma'am?"

"I am Grass Woman, the third wife of Many Horses, the man who led the war party. I spoke to you yesterday when they brought you here."

Lewallen asked, "What're they going to do with me and my sister, Eula Bee? Are they going to kill me because I wounded the Kiowa?"

She said quietly, "No, they won't kill you. The People think you are very brave because you shot a raider on your farm and because you attacked a warrior just now. The war party heard your singing on the way to our camp. Captives of Comanches do not sing as they ride. That was most brave also."

"Where's my sister, ma'am?"

"My husband has decided that the peace chief will have her. The peace chief is Yellow Wolf. My husband, Many Horses, will give your sister to Yellow Wolf and the Mexican girl along with her. As the chief of the war party, it is my husband's right to give away the captives he has brought back. Many Horses will give cattle and horses to the other raiders. Though the Kiowa asked to be awarded your sister, Many Horses plans to give her to Yellow Wolf. He will give the Mexican boy to Small Buffalo."

"Small Buffalo?"

"Yes, he is the Kiowa."

Lewallen stumbled to his feet in a rage. "That Kiowa wanted my sister? He's the one who had the scalps of my ma and brother and uncle, so I guess he's the one who killed them."

"Yes, if he has their scalps, that would be so. Small Buffalo seeks to become a great warrior of the Kiowa tribe. He wants to wear the red sash of the bravest Kiowas, as his father does. Small Buffalo has married the oldest daughter of Yellow Wolf. The Kiowa is favored by the peace chief."

Lewallen sank back down to his knees. The strength had all at once drained out of him. He hastily rubbed away the tears that came flooding to his eyes and told her, "I hope that Kiowa won't ever be able to raid any settlers again because of what I did to him just now."

There was no answer from the woman, only silence.

Lewallen was quiet, too, for a time, thinking about this kind lady. He decided he ought to be polite and ask her about herself. "Are you a Texan, too, ma'am?"

"Once I was."

"How long have you been here? Where did they get hold of you?"

"I think I've been among The People for nearly ten years. It seems strange to speak English again. I haven't had anyone to speak English to since my cousin who was captured with me died winter before last. We were traveling in a covered wagon to my grandfather's in Oregon when the Indians attacked our wagon train. Tell me, who is the president of the United States now?"

"A man by the name of Abraham Lincoln, and because of him we're fighting a Civil War back East and my pa's gone off to fight in it. Ma'am, are you the only other prisoner in this camp besides me, my sister, and the Cabrals?"

"No, there are some Mexican women who've been here longer than I have. Yellow Wolf's second wife was a Mexican captive. She can speak with the Mexican child if she can recall their language."

Lewallen sat down and clasped his knees with his arms, rubbing his cheek against one trousered knee. The feel of the cloth comforted him. "What about me? Who gets me?" he asked next.

"You belong to my husband. What did Many Horses say when you came up to him after you'd attacked Small Buffalo? As a woman I dared not come close enough to the two chiefs to hear."

Lewallen reflected a moment, then said, "It was short, only one word. It sounded like 'two' more than anything else."

"Ah, I think he said *tsaa*. That means 'good.' My husband liked the way you sang on your way here. I am sure that he plans to keep you for himself. I would like that, too. What is your name?"

"Lewallen, Lewallen Collier, from Palo Duro. My sister's name is Eula Beatrice, but we call her Eula Bee."

"I was Mary Jane Hankins before I became Grass Woman."

Lewallen told her, "I'm truly sorry, ma'am, that you've been here so long with the Indians. When my pa and big brother come back from fighting the War, they'll come riding here and rescue all of us captives from the Comanches."

"Perhaps they will do that, Lewallen, but I doubt it." Her next words were calm and measured. "You are a slave now."

"A slave?" Tomás had been dead right. The ugly word stung Lewallen to the quick. He demanded, "What about my sister? Will she have to be a slave, too? She ain't big enough yet to do much work."

"I don't know. She's very small, and so is the Mexican girl. The wives of Yellow Wolf like girl children. I think your sister and the Mexican girl will become daughters of The People."

"The People? You mean the Comanches?"

"Yes. That is what we call ourselves. I think that your sister is still young enough to forget the white man's ways."

"Eula Bee won't ever forget anything about who she is —a Collier!"

Grass Woman's words were gentle. "No, you speak for yourself. You will never forget because, like me, you are old enough to remember."

Lewallen growled, "I won't be a slave for anybody, not for long anyhow. I'll escape as soon as I can. Just you wait and see."

"I dare not help you, Lewallen Collier."

"With all due respect, ma'am, and thank you for your kindness, but I ain't asking for your help. I'll come back and save Eula Bee if I can't take her with me when I go. And if I come back, I'll come back with Texas Rangers or somebody. And then I'll save you, too."

"No, Lewallen. I am the wife of Many Horses now, not Mary Jane Hankins. My husband is of The People and so am I. If white men came seeking me by my old name, I would not go willingly with them. My husband paid twelve ponies to my Indian parents to make me his wife. I will not shame him by leaving him."

Lewallen muttered, "Your People even killed our dog just before they killed my kinfolk."

The woman's voice grew louder. "No Comanche did

that! The dog is sacred to us. If your dog was killed, the Kiowa brave was the one who did it."

"Him again? Small Buffalo. That doesn't surprise me. He killed my ma and her old uncle and my brother Daniel, too, and because of that I hate Small Buffalo more than you could ever believe. I hope I killed him when I cut him with the knife."

"You took him by surprise and wounded him. He'll remember these things and remember you, but he will not die from some slashes from a knife held by a boy. Small Buffalo is young and very strong."

Lewallen muttered angrily, "I guess he won't. He's too mean. How could that Kiowa want my sister after he killed her mother and brother? I don't understand. Does he want to kill her, too? He sure tried to kill me, and if your husband hadn't stopped him, he would have."

"I know, Lewallen. Many Horses told me how he saved you because of your courage. Small Buffalo wants your sister to come to his lodge because he has no children. Snow Moon, his wife, bore a child to him who died of a choking sickness last spring. She weeps for the child." Grass Woman sighed deeply. "I have no children either now." Rising to her feet, she asked, "Lewallen, are you hungry?"

"Yes, ma'am, I guess I am. Thank you."

FOUR

The Camp

In the days that followed Lewallen would have been lost and utterly miserable except for the ever-present companionship of Grass Woman. She was the one, the third wife of the powerful Many Horses, who gave him his instructions and showed him what labor was expected of a captive boy-slave. Many Horses paid little heed to him, nor did the raider's first wife, though Lewallen was at times aware of the war chief's eyes on him.

He worked side by side with Grass Woman and Many Horses' second wife, plump, little Holds the Arrows, who had a happy nature. The work Lewallen did was considered women's work by the Indians. But he found it to be very hard, the sort of work his father or Johnny would have done on their farm, not his mother. It wasn't only heavy work; it was constant. There wasn't much time for him to grieve for his family because he was seldom alone, and he held to his vow not to cry unless he could cry unobserved.

Hunting, making war, fashioning bows, arrows, shields, and lances was the labor of the men, but Lewallen learned soon that the women did everything else. They skinned the animals the men killed and tanned the hides, soaking them, scraping off the hair, and stretching the skin, to make lodge covers, bags, and clothing. They gathered mesquite beans, pecan nuts, and fruit and berries in season, and they laboriously pounded the meat and fruit together to make dry food to be packed into bags for winter rations.

The Comanche women were never idle, although the men who weren't hunting gambled, raced ponies, lounged about on buffalo robes, or rode through the camp showing off the fine clothing the women had made them.

Lewallen had been a captive in Many Horses' lodge for less than a month when, one morning, he spotted Eula Bee riding by on a black-and-white pony. His sister looked frightened and was hanging on hard to the pony's mane. Afraid that he would startle her and she would fall, Lewallen did not dare to call out to her from where he knelt beside Holds the Arrows and Grass Woman, as they scraped the hide of a deer Many Horses had killed.

Grass Woman noticed his concern. She looked toward his sister and said, "Yellow Wolf has given the horse to your sister, the *ekapi*, the redhead, whose nature pleases him. He thinks her spirit is as bold as yours. He says she will marry a great chief someday because she no longer weeps at night."

Lewallen bit back the words, "No, she won't marry any Indian!" and bent resentfully to his work again.

Days went by before he set eyes on Eula Bee again. It was as if the Comanches had decided he shouldn't speak with her. Each time he saw her outside she was with one of the wives of Yellow Wolf and almost always in the company of Angelita, who had a pony like Eula Bee's. Though he couldn't talk with Eula Bee, he did the one thing he could to let her know that he was there in the camp: he whistled "Lorena." Each time he did the Indians stopped whatever they were doing to stare at him.

Lewallen called out once to Eula Bee when she came very close to him as she played kickball with some older Indian girls and Angelita. She waved her hand at him and cried out, "Lewtie," but then was grabbed by the arm and shaken by one of the older girls and hurried away to a lodge out of his sight. Disappointed, Lewallen comforted himself with the knowledge that she'd looked well fed and certainly was well dressed. Yellow Wolf's wives had made her a little dress of fringed doeskin with red and blue beads on its yoke and little beaded moccasins. Angelita was dressed in exactly the same way. In her Comanche clothing black-haired Angelita looked like an Indian but not Eula Bee, whose curling, red mane showed like fire during the kickball game.

Some days later Grass Woman spoke to him of Eula Bee while he helped her cut up venison for the stew kettle. "Do not go near Yellow Wolf's lodges, Lewallen. Do not seek your sister out. It is forbidden to you."

"Forbidden." The word stung like a burr in Lewallen's mind. He'd been right; they were keeping his sister away from him. All right, he'd keep his distance from Eula Bee, but he'd go right on whistling "Lorena" for her sake. And come hell or high water he planned to try to talk to her before he escaped.

Even though he was kept apart from Eula Bee, he sometimes saw Tomás Cabral because both boys worked with the women, and at times all of the women of the band went out together plum picking. One day late that summer Small Buffalo's slender little wife Snow Moon went out with the others, and Tomás, her husband's slave, went with her. Lewallen's eyes met Tomás's on the way, and an unspoken message passed between the two of them.

So when Grass Woman and Holds the Arrows were out of hearing on the other side of a bush by the river, Lewallen edged close enough to Tomás to talk with him. He didn't waste time asking him about Small Buffalo's health because he'd seen the Kiowa riding around the camp, proudly but bandaged, about a week after he'd attacked him. Small Buffalo had given Lewallen one burning glance, then looked away as if to prove to the warrior riding with him that a slave was beneath his notice. He hadn't sought revenge through the Comanche chiefs, probably because Lewallen was so much beneath his dignity that it would lower him to do so. Yet the glance the young brave had given him had been one of bitter hatred, and Lewallen had returned it.

Lewallen asked hurriedly, "Tom, do they treat you all right? Does Small Buffalo hit you or whip you?"

"No, they treat me all right. I try to work hard and fast enough to please Snow Moon. Small Buffalo pays no heed to me. He is more interested in having his wife brush and oil his hair. After all, I did not count *coup* on him as you did."

"What's that?"

"Touching someone with your hand. That is more important to the Comanches than shooting an arrow into an enemy. You must come very close to touch the enemy. Small Buffalo says he touched you once in battle, and then here in camp you touched him. The Comanches cry out *a-he* when they touch someone. It is greater than taking a scalp to count *coup*—to touch your enemy."

"Mmm," mumbled Lewallen, remembering how the Kiowa had touched him as he'd galloped by during the attack. He asked, "How do you know what Small Buffalo says to people?"

"Because one of the wives of Yellow Wolf is a Mexican. She speaks to Angelita and me in Spanish. The Comanches like to have people in their camps who can speak Spanish. Such people are useful."

Lewallen didn't ask why. Instead he wanted to know, "Do they let you talk to your sister?"

"No, they keep me away from her."

"They keep me away from Eula Bee, too. They want to make Comanches out of the girls." Lewallen nudged Tomás on the arm and whispered, stepping nearer, "Tom, have you been thinking about escaping?"

"Yes, but they watch me." The dark-haired boy shook his head mournfully.

"Me, too. Day and night. Grass Woman ties a leather rope to me at night. She ties mean knots, and she sleeps with one eye open and the other end of the rope tied to her wrist."

"Yes, Snow Moon ties me up, too."

"If you can think of a good way to escape, Tom, will you let me know what it is?"

"Yes, if I find the chance to talk with you again, Lewallen. Are you learning any of the Comanche language?"

"Yep, I can't help but learn some of it, hearing it all the time."

Tomás shook his head. "Small Buffalo knows no Spanish, but a few of the other men seem to. I talked with two of them once and told them that they should not have come to our land, but they were not shamed by my words. They said our farm was a Mexican farm, and they raid Mexican settlements."

Tomás would have continued, but just then they heard Grass Woman calling, "Lewallen." Tomás stuck out his hand and gripped Lewallen's hard. "Thank you for not fighting with your knife that day."

"Thanks for warning me to act brave, Tom. If we can't get away from here together, I'll come back and save you, along with Eula Bee and your sister."

Swiftly Tomás nodded and asked, "Do you know what the Indians call you? Yellow Wolf's wife told me in Spanish what it was."

"No, what is it?"

"Sings His War Song."

"What?"

Tomás released his hand and hurried off as Grass Woman came up from around the bush with a woven basket, which she pushed into Lewallen's arms. She looked at him strangely when he started to laugh, but she said nothing.

He'd figured out what Tomás had just told him. The Indians must be referring to his constant singing and whistling of "Lorena." It was a love song, not a war chant, but his singing of it on the trail and in the camp to remind Eula Bee that he was there must have made the Comanches think it was a white man's war song. And, come to think of it, Many Horses had been impressed with his singing on the way to the camp. Grass Woman had told him so a long time ago.

While he carried the basket back to the camp later, Lewallen confessed to himself something he wouldn't have believed last spring. There was good stuff, lots of it, in Tomás Cabral. He was smart, too. Look at the things he knew. Daniel had spotted the worth of Tomás, which was why they'd been friends. Lewallen wished now that he'd talked with him and Daniel and learned some of the Indian things Tomás's father had told him.

A few days later the council of leaders decided to move the camp. A herald rode through the nine-mile-long string of lodges, calling out when they would leave and what sort of country they'd be going to next.

Grass Woman scurried about now, giving chirping orders to Lewallen to help her take down the buffalo-skin lodge and pack it.

"What's happening?" Lewallen asked her, as he still didn't know enough of the language to understand what the herald had been shouting.

"We're going to another camp, where many berries are ripe now. We go each year when the fruit is ripe. It is the way of The People."

So they broke camp the next morning, led by Yellow Wolf, trailed by several hundred riders. The Collier horse that had brought Lewallen to Yellow Wolf's camp had been awarded by Many Horses to one of the warriors who had gone on the war party. Now as they set off to the new camp Lewallen rode beside Grass Woman on an Indian pony, an old slow beast that he knew all too well would never be any means of escape. Not only was the pony too old and slow, he was surrounded by Indians on every side.

Once he'd made certain that Eula Bee was riding safely on her own pony in Yellow Wolf's family group, Lewallen turned his attention to the country they were traveling through. He fixed the location of the camp they were leaving in his mind just as he'd tried to remember landmarks in the country he'd passed through with the war party. There had been creeks along the way and that gap in the range of hills and a few others things. He could also recall where the sun had been when they'd come to various points, so he had some idea how long it took a pony to get from place to place at a steady trot.

Two days' ride to the north brought the Comanches to a spectacular landmark, a wide, muddy, red river, flowing west and east. Because its waters had diminished in the summer drought, the Indians slid down its banks and forded it easily without losing any ponies to suck holes. In spring it would not be so safe, according to Grass Woman.

They made a new camp a day's ride beyond this river. To Lewallen's way of thinking this new one was much like the old—lodges of buffalo skin clustered together in family groups, strung out along the edge of a creek. The creek wound lazily through bushy meadows and stands of fruit-bearing trees. As before, the new camp was busy, noisy, and dog-infested, although it lay amid beautiful surroundings.

Lewallen helped Grass Woman and the other wives set

up Many Horses' tepees close to the tepees of Yellow Wolf. This location was a very great honor for Many Horses, and Grass Woman told Lewallen proudly that it was because of the successful raid he had led. Hearing her boasting made Lewallen think bitterly of his murdered family, of his and Eula Bee's captivity, and of the Collier cattle and mare the Indians had stolen. Their old milk cow was long gone. Because she couldn't keep up with the Comanche ponies and stolen cattle, the Indians had left her to die of thirst on the prairie the second day of their march to the camp where Lewallen had met Grass Woman.

He was wary of Grass Woman. Though she'd helped him when he'd been frightened and upset and he was grateful for that, he knew at bottom she was a Comanche. Grass Woman had been some years older than Eula Bee when taken prisoner, but by now The People had claimed her almost totally. No, this wasn't going to happen to Eula Bee, not as long as he had breath in his body to sing or whistle "Lorena" whenever he thought she could hear him. He had to be wary of that, too, because twice when he'd spotted her and started to sing, the Comanche girls had caught her by the shoulders and hustled her off. The second time Yellow Wolf's oldest wife had held Eula Bee's head so she couldn't look at him, which had stopped the words in his throat.

He got to talk at times with Tomás, though, because Small Buffalo's and Many Horses' tepees were so close together. One day as he watched the lodge of the young Kiowa he saw Tomás crawl out with a leather water bag and head toward the creek. Lewallen followed him, taking along a gourd to fill.

As the two boys knelt side by side lowering the bag and gourd into the stream, Lewallen whispered to Tom, "Did you think of a way to escape yet?"

"Yes, I have. But I cannot do it. I cannot get the trust of Small Buffalo. I am told he does not trust Mexicans."

"Why do you have to have him trust you, Tom?"

"So he will set me to guarding his ponies with the other Comanche boys. You must have a pony to escape."

"Ponies?" Lewallen's eyes narrowed. Yes, there were always people with the Comanche ponies, keeping an eye on them while they grazed away from the camp. Indian ponies never roamed loose.

Tomás went on, speaking softly. "My father escaped the Indians in this way a long time ago."

Lewallen only nodded impatiently, then asked, "Do you think the Texas Rangers or somebody like them could be hunting for us right now, Tom?"

"No. I do not think so. They may not know what band took us or where we are now. But there is another reason why. There is the War."

"Yes," Lewallen mumbled angrily. If it wasn't for the danged War, he was sure his pa and Johnny would have tracked him and Eula Bee by now and rescued them. Even better, the two men would have fought off the Indians when they came to attack the farm in the first place.

Quickly he got to his feet with the filled gourd and said, "Good luck, Tom," because Snow Moon had come up behind Tomás and was staring suspiciously at both of them as they whispered together.

Lewallen nodded to her and ambled off whistling "Lorena." Eula Bee wasn't anywhere in sight, but maybe she'd hear it all the same.

Lewallen learned from Grass Woman that—once they'd picked all the food they could here—the next camp of The People would be close to buffalo country. The aim of Yellow Wolf's band would be to get meat for the winter that lay ahead. Now that autumn was drawing near, Grass Woman said that the buffalo were becoming lazy, fat, and slow from their summer-long, rich grazing.

Lewallen had hoped that Small Buffalo might tire of Tom and return him to Many Horses, but the Kiowa didn't. Small Buffalo kept his slave, and he, too, stayed among the Comanches. He asked Grass Woman once why Small Buffalo, who after all was only a visitor, stayed so long and didn't go to his own tribe. She told him that his wife, Snow Moon, was going to have her second baby in late winter, and she wanted to stay in her father's lodge until the baby was born. Her husband respected her wishes, and besides he enjoyed being among The People, where he was greatly admired.

Lewallen had been rankled by Small Buffalo's presence but had hidden his feelings. He had no intention of attacking him again. He knew he'd be severely punished, if not killed, for doing so this time. Grass Woman had even hinted at this as she warned him in her careful way. Yet Lewallen hated the Indian dandy, from the soles of his quill-adorned moccasins to the two crow feathers at the top of his sleek head. He didn't want to lose Tomás as a friend, but he'd sure like to see the last of Small Buffalo.

FIVE

Buffalo Autumn

Yellow Wolf's band rode southwest in early September at a very leisurely pace, stopping each night where they could find water or a sheltered spot from the winds. Young men mounted on fast ponies went out each dawn from the camp in various directions to scout for two things—buffalo herds and a good place to set up a hunting camp. The camp had to be in a wooded area near a stream, Grass Woman explained to Lewallen. Mounted beside him, she told him that they must have wood in plenty to build frames for stretching the buffalo hides.

During the fifth sunset of the slow-moving journey over the plains, Lewallen heard wild shouting and then saw a young brave galloping over the grass from the west. Lewallen knew the word he was crying because he'd heard it used over and over among the Comanches. *Tasiwoo!* To him it sounded silly, but to the Indians it meant something vital to their way of life—"buffalo."

The scout brought the welcome news that there was a great herd of the animals and a good spot for a camp only one hard day's ride from where they were now.

❀ ❀ ❀

"This is good fortune, finding a herd so easily," Grass Woman told Lewallen the next evening, as he helped her put up the horizontal tent the Indians used in hunting camps instead of tepees.

Then she told him, as he dug the pit for their cook fire, "Many Horses does not hunt buffalo with a bow as the others do, and he scorns the pistol he took from you. He does not run the animals over a cliff to die either. He uses a lance." She was quiet for a moment, then went on, "Many Horses has told me to tell you that he wishes you to go to the hunt with him."

"Does he want me to hunt, too? Is he going to give me a pony and a rifle?" Was this a way to escape? Lewallen asked himself. He'd never seen a buffalo hunt, though he'd hunted on foot with his brothers back home for deer and antelope.

"No, he will not give you a weapon. He says that you are only to come with him and see the hunting because he thinks someday you, too, may hunt as a man of The People, as a Comanche warrior."

Lewallen held back the angry retort that he would never become a Comanche. Instead he asked, "Will Small Buffalo hunt with the Comanches, too?"

"Certainly he will. He is a fine hunter."

"I was pretty sure he would be," Lewallen muttered. "I suppose the things Small Buffalo does here with the Comanches will make him a red-sash man someday with his own tribe, too, huh?" He'd heard a great deal from her about the importance of such a brave among the Kiowas. Only ten men of a Kiowa band were permitted to wear a red sash.

"Yes, they may. His deeds here will be told to the Kiowas, and a record is kept of them by Yellow Wolf and the others."

"Like killing my poor old uncle and my ma and my little brother?"

Grass Woman didn't look at him as she said, "Lewallen, the white men have killed many, many Indian women and children as well as men."

"I never heard about any!" he protested.

"It is not a thing white men would boast about to their families."

Lewallen turned his head from her so she couldn't see his face by the just-kindled firelight and the look of disbelief on it. Under his breath he let out a long string of his favorite cuss words. Sure enough, Small Buffalo would be out for glory on the hunt. He hoped maybe a buffalo would get even with him for the sake of the Colliers, but he knew that wasn't likely to happen.

That night the Comanches danced their hunting dance. Then Yellow Wolf led the hunters out early the next morning, following the same scout who had brought the news of the herd. Mounted Comanche-style on a chunky, dun-colored pony, Lewallen rode off behind his master, Many Horses.

Grass Woman had given Lewallen his instructions from her husband. He was to stay away from the buffalo herd but keep his eyes fixed on the hunters, to watch and learn from them. She and other women from the hunting camp would follow the men at a slower pace and arrive later in the day at the hunting ground to help butcher the buffalo.

The hunters rode west for some hours over the prairie in the cool winds of the autumn morning under a sky of cloudless blue. The high, yellow grass bent and rippled under the wind; sometimes as the Indians passed antelope flicked the white part of their rears to alert the others to danger and bounded away.

Like the Indians, Lewallen rode bareback with his knees under a coil of leather rope tied onto the pony. Like them he rode naked except for a breechclout. He'd left his trousers back at the camp, along with the new buckskin shirt Grass woman had sewn for him to replace his cambric one. His old boots had worn out so he now wore moccasins. Except for his unbraided brown hair and white skin, he looked much like a Comanche. He was embarrassed by his near nakedness and very much aware of his gooseflesh among the muscular, copper-bodied warriors. At times he felt the eyes of the hunters upon him, and he'd look away rather than meet their gaze. He hoped no one would try to talk with him. Although he could sometimes catch the drift of a Comanche conversation, he couldn't speak the language.

But he need not have had any fear of anyone trying to talk with him. No one spoke at all. Yellow Wolf and the buffalo scout led the party, which rode in such silence Lewallen could scarcely believe it. The scout flung up his arm near midday at the base of a line of low hills. He dismounted and in company with Yellow Wolf climbed to a hilltop where they lay down for a time. Then the two Indians returned to mount up again.

As all of them moved forward, urging their ponies up the slope, Many Horses turned around to look at Lewallen and pointed to the sky, where ravens were wheeling about

on the other side of the hill. The Comanche lifted his hunting lance and shook it, making Lewallen guess rightly: the
presence of ravens was a sign that buffalo were nearby.
Yes, Many Horses did intend to teach him about hunting.
This was his first lesson.

Lewallen was pondering it when all at once he heard a
whooping sound from the summit of the hill. The hunt had
begun with Yellow Wolf's first whoop. The Comanche
ponies poured over the hilltop, then slid down the other
side. All of the hunters shouted, screeched, and whooped,
except for Lewallen, who was struck dumb with wonder at
what he saw on the prairie below him.

It seemed to him that there was nothing for miles on end
but the huge bodies of thousands and thousands of brown-
black, heavy-headed buffalo.

He would have stayed behind the hunt, as Grass Woman
had told him to do, in order to watch the hunters and
marvel at the buffalo, but as the Indian ponies galloped
forward on level ground, Lewallen's dun took off in swift
pursuit. The dun seemed to have a mind of its own. No
matter how hard he pulled on the rein, it wouldn't halt for
him. The horse didn't know the meaning of the word *whoa*.

The alarmed buffalo had begun to run the instant they'd
heard the yelling of the Comanches, but the heavy beasts
weren't as fast or nimble as the Indian ponies, which had
been trained as buffalo-hunting mounts. Each Indian, once
he was inside the galloping herd, chose one buffalo to kill,
and in spite of the enormous clouds of dust the running
buffalo made on the dry plain, the Comanche brave stuck
close to that buffalo, always riding up on its right side.

Lewallen's pony had gone on many buffalo hunts, and

it must have felt that it was to hunt, too. It knew the pony Many Horses rode as a herd companion from the pasture, so the dun followed each and every twist and turn that Many Horses' pinto made among the earthshaking, stampeding buffalo and yelling Comanches. There were other Indian ponies on either side of Many Horses' pinto, but Lewallen's mount paid no heed to them, only to the pinto directly ahead.

Lewallen gritted his teeth, bent over, and hung on to the neck of his mount as it galloped among the buffalo that were so close he could count *coup* on them. Through the high-rising, yellow dust he saw Many Horses just behind a bull buffalo. He was riding with his lance held across his body. Suddenly the Comanche's experienced hunting pony leaped forward in a burst of speed until its head was just behind the head of the running buffalo. Then Many Horses took his lance in both hands and shoved it down into the side of the buffalo bull, aiming for its heart. The buffalo, with the lance sticking in him, tried to swerve to gore the pony with his horns, but Many Horses thrust the lance deeper into his side, and as the buffalo fell the Comanche let go of the lance and his pony darted past it.

Lewallen's dun followed, leaping over the body of the dead buffalo, still galloping after Many Horses' pinto. Lewallen shouted in fright, but over the screeching of the Indians killing buffalo with their bows and pistols, no one heard him. And then as he raised his head to gasp for breath in the choking dust, he saw Many Horses' pony fall, rump over head, throwing the Comanche to the ground, its front hoof caught in a prairie-dog hole.

Many Horses bounded to his feet to face the herd and

stood for a long moment as the panic-stricken buffalo came running at him, parting to his left and right, to avoid colliding with Lewallen's pony. Lewallen saw the flash of the chief's eyes, seeking his, as the dun pony raced toward him, and he saw the Indian's hand outstretched to him.

Without thinking of his own safety or of anything but the hundreds of buffalo thundering behind him, Lewallen reached his left hand out and down to Many Horses.

He caught Lewallen's hand and holding it leaped up into the air, nearly jerking him off his pony. Then he settled with a thud atop the dun behind Lewallen. Carrying a double burden now, the pony raced out ahead of the buffalo as the herd came in a tumult of hooves over the body of the screaming pony, which had broken its leg, pounding it into the earth in a trampled mass.

Lewallen felt the strong arm of Many Horses about his waist and the man's hands on the one rein, guiding the racing dun in front of the herd to the south and finally galloping out of it to its fringes. Once they were out of the herd entirely, the Comanche reined in, and he and Lewallen sat together on the weary pony, looking toward the stampeding buffalo. Though wild shoutings arose from the herd, which proved to Lewallen that the Comanches were still hunting, he could see nothing at all but a great cloud of yellow-brown dust and occasionally a dark nightmare-shaped mass hurtling by inside the cloud.

He became aware in spite of his shivering that Many Horses had put his hand on his right shoulder, and he heard him say, "*Tsaa. Tsaa,*" which he knew meant "Good. Good." He also added "*Pekha tasiwoo.*" Many Horses had said that he had "killed the buffalo." Lewallen was glad to hear praise for his behavior.

Then Many Horses said one word only, *"Haints."*

The word, which was Comanche for "friend," burst in his head. Many Horses seemed to be calling him friend.

Hope rose in Lewallen's heart that this act, which had been more the result of instinct than anything else, would somehow help him to escape. Had he won the trust of Many Horses today? He prayed that he had.

Once the buffalo had passed, Many Horses and Lewallen rode back to the scene of the hunt. The prairie was peppered with the great bodies of the animals and the Comanches riding among them, each man looking for his own specially marked arrows that would identify his kill.

Since only Many Horses had used a lance, it was a simple matter to identify his bull. After dismounting, Lewallen stood beside the dead beast, marveling at its bulk and wondering how the Indians would handle its large carcass.

By midafternoon he'd witnessed the Comanche manner of butchering a buffalo. It amazed him. As soon as the rest of Yellow Wolf's band appeared on the prairie, the women and the men started to work. Each family attended to its own buffalo.

Many Horses, his three wives, and Lewallen, all grunting with effort, heaved the buffalo onto its stomach with its legs spread wide. Then, on the command of Many Horses delivered through Grass Woman, Lewallen stood back to watch. The Comanche chief wielded a skinning knife with as much skill as his wives. Within minutes the four of them had the hide peeled back down the middle of the spine and the forequarters removed. Soon the hindquarters were taken off, and the flank and brisket were sliced off in one piece of meat. The entrails were removed, and rib steaks torn away from the spine by hand.

In only two hours' time there was nothing remaining of the bull but the skeleton, slender rump, and the massive head. The buffalo's heart was left in the bloody rib cage as a magical offering. Not all of the meat, however, was packed into the wet hide and loaded onto the pack ponies Many Horses' wives had brought with them. Some of the meat was devoured on the spot. But Lewallen couldn't bring himself to eat any of the raw liver, brains, or bone marrow.

Because of the haste in the butchering, Lewallen had no chance to talk with Grass Woman about the hunt, and he'd noticed that Many Horses seldom spoke to her either, except to give orders.

He wondered if Many Horses would tell her about the fall, though surely others would notice that his pinto pony was gone. What would Many Horses say and how would he say it?

That evening, back at the hunting camp, while two of Many Horses' wives were roasting buffalo steaks over the fires, Grass Woman came to Lewallen and told him excitedly, "My husband has said that you came to his aid when his pony fell. If you were a boy of The People, he would give a dance in your honor. It was a very fine thing you did."

Lewallen said, "The buffalo would have run him down under their hooves."

"Many a man of our tribe has died that way. I am very happy that you saved my husband. He trusts you now. He says you ride well and can manage horses and were so eager to become a hunter of buffalo that you sent your pony into the herd even though you had no weapon. He says because of your deed that he is going to take you away from doing women's work and send you to herd his ponies. He has thirty-one ponies."

Herding the Comanche ponies! Lewallen felt his heart begin to beat harder. Trying to act pleased and still be calm, he asked, "When will I start?"

"When we have gone to our winter camp. Until then you will help me dry the meat in the sun for the winter and peg the hides here while the men hunt more buffalo."

Lewallen asked, "Did anybody else see what happened when his pinto stumbled?"

"No one did, but my husband plans to praise your brave deed at the buffalo-tongue feast Yellow Wolf is going to give tomorrow morning."

Lewallen snorted. "Small Buffalo sure isn't going to like hearing that. It might take some glory away from him."

Grass Woman shook her head. "He killed three buffalo today. He is generous. He gave the meat and hides of two of them to men of our band who have grown too old to hunt for themselves. This makes him popular, and Yellow Wolf favors him."

Lewallen sighed, then set his thoughts to the important thing she had told him. He was to herd Many Horses' ponies!

Two full moons passed before the Comanches left the

buffalo plains to set up their lodges in the winter camp.

By this time Lewallen had noticed something unusual. There were very few small children in this Indian band. He'd asked Grass Woman about it and had been told that not many babies were born, and of those that were a large number died as infants. Many Horses had fathered five children, and all had died. There was much sickness and many accidents. Because there were so few children they were greatly valued. They sometimes purchased children from poorer Indian tribes by giving ponies for them. They raised these children as Comanches, and they very often adopted captive children.

Grass Woman told Lewallen once, as they pegged down a buffalo hide together, "We think it is evil for a parent to strike his child. I remember how I was beaten with a stick by my mother before I came to live here."

He pondered her words after she'd gone off to another chore, leaving him to pull the hide taut against the pegs. Her words stung him. Eula Bee didn't seem to be unhappy nowadays nor did Angelita. Every time he saw them they were laughing and playing with Comanche girls in the hunting camp. And his sister didn't turn her head toward him when he whistled "Lorena" anymore. It was almost as if she didn't hear the song.

On their last morning at the hunting camp, while the Indians were busily loading the pack ponies with their gear, Lewallen slipped over to Small Buffalo's part of the camp to talk with Tom. By luck he found him alone, down on his knees, fastening the thongs of one of the leather rolls the Indians carried their clothing in.

He whispered, "Tom, I might not get to talk to you

again, but I hear that Many Horses is going to send me out to guard his ponies pretty soon. When he does, I'm going to try to cut out the fastest pony and escape before the snow comes. Then, somehow, I'm going to come back."

"Yes." Tom looked over his shoulder to where Snow Moon was adjusting a bundle of hides on a travois. Her back was turned to them, so he went on hastily, "The fastest pony is the black one that belongs to Small Buffalo. He boasts over and over that it has won many races for him. I know enough Comanche now to understand Small Buffalo."

"Good, Tom. I know the pony. I'll take it then." Lawallen's face wore its first truly wide grin in months. "The Indians stole our horses, so I'll steal one of theirs. That evens things up a bit, doesn't it?"

"Do you think you know the way back?" Tomás asked anxiously.

"I think I do. I kept track of the landmarks wherever we went." Lewallen eyed Snow Moon nervously. She might turn around at any moment and catch him talking to her slave. He said hastily, "Tom, if I don't get a chance to say good-bye to Eula Bee, will you tell her I've gone to get help? Tell her I plan to come back. Do you promise me that?"

"I promise."

"Thank you. Tell my sister to wait for me and watch for me. I promised Pa that I'd look out for Eula Bee, and that's what Ma would've wanted me to do, too."

SIX

Away!

Yellow Wolf's winter camp lay, according to Grass Woman, to the north and west of the buffalo grounds. It would take them four days to reach it. As Lewallen rode behind her and the other wives of Many Horses, he kept his eyes on the countryside about him even more than he did on Eula Bee, who was riding with the peace chief's family. There were plenty of memorable landmarks on the way to the winter camp, which lay on higher ground. Grass Woman said there would be high bluffs before they came to it and wide meadows and fields among the hills that would shelter the camp, which was to be set up in a canyon.

As they crossed a particularly large meadow, Grass Woman turned around on her pony and spoke to Lewallen. "This camp we go to now is a good place. It is a new one. My husband found it while chasing a deer two springs ago. He has told Yellow Wolf that this meadow will be good pasture for the ponies of the band."

The ponies! Lewallen's eyes examined the meadow with great care, and he saw that it was really two meadows in one—divided north and south by a jumble of enormous boulders. He drew in his breath, thinking. The boulders could be a big help to his plans.

A few miles farther on they entered the canyon, and as Grass Woman had said it was a good place, with tree-rimmed rock walls and a creek meandering through the bottom. The walls were high enough to give the lodges shelter from the icy winds that would later come blowing in from the plains. The spot would be as good as any, and a lot better than most, for Eula Bee. He needn't worry about her freezing here. What's more, as the pet of Yellow Wolf's lodge, she wouldn't suffer for her brother's actions after he'd escaped.

For two days he served Grass Woman and Many Horses' other wives, helping to set up their lodges for the long winter, bringing wood to them, and doing the other chores required for a long stay. When everything was done to the women's satisfaction, he went to Grass Woman and told her, "I am ready to start herding ponies now."

"Yes." She nodded at Lewallen. "I will ask my husband when he wishes you to start going out with the other boys." She smiled and added, "It is an honor he shows you, Lewallen."

"Yes, ma'am."

That evening for the first time she didn't tie Lewallen to her with the rope when they lay down to sleep, and she told him, "Many Horses has said that he is sending you out with his ponies tomorrow."

Tomorrow! That was good—the sooner the better because of the coming winter. Lewallen lay in the darkness of the tepee, listening to Grass Woman's soft breathing, thinking, wondering what lay ahead for her and for the two Cabrals, Eula Bee, and himself. What if he failed in what he hoped to do? What if he was recaptured and killed? The danger would be great. He gnawed in silence on the back of his hand in an agony of apprehension until at last sleep overtook him.

That next morning, a chilly one of dry-leaf autumn, Lewallen took up his welcome duty as a herdsman to Many Horses' thirty-one ponies. Like the other boys, he was to guard the animals from wolves and panthers and horse-raiding Indians from other tribes. Herding ponies was a very responsible job for a young Comanche, a step along the road that led to becoming a brave. All of the men of the tribe had been herdsmen as youths, and many had become very great warriors. Grass Woman had told him so.

After he mounted the same dun he'd ridden on the buffalo hunt, she gave him a skin bag of water, a knife, and a small pouch of dried meat. "My husband trusts you, Lewallen Collier," she said.

He told her, "Don't you fret, ma'am. Nothing bad is going to happen to his ponies while I'm around them."

After all, it was the Kiowa's black pony he had designs on—not any of Many Horses' animals.

Grass Woman caught him by the ankle before he could ride out after the ponies Many Horses' first wife had just let out of the wooden pen built to hold them overnight. "Don't think you'll be able to run away," she told him. "There are no better trackers than our warriors. I have not forgotten what you told me that time I first talked to you."

Lewallen just grinned down at her and said, "I'll bet that's true—that they're jim-dandy trackers," as she released his ankle.

As he rode out of camp he whistled "Lorena," then sang it at the top of his lungs, hoping the song would bring Eula Bee out of Yellow Wolf's lodge so he could at least wave good-bye to her.

But he saw only Tom Cabral. He was down by the creek using sand to scour out an iron kettle for Snow Woman, and as Lewallen passed him, he gazed questioningly at him. Lewallen gave him a nod. Yes, today was the day! Tom nodded in return, then went back to his scouring. Lewallen knew that he would tell Eula Bee in secret what he'd promised to. Tom was plenty smart. It was too bad he wasn't riding out with him right now.

The other boys were also on their way to the grazing meadows this morning. Yellow Wolf's and Small Buffalo's ponies were tended by one boy, a thickset twelve-year-old Lewallen knew by sight. The boy had turned friendly ever since Many Horses had praised Lewallen at the buffalo-tongue feast. He'd tried once or twice to talk to Lewallen, but they couldn't get through to each other because of the different languages. Now, once they'd arrived at the double meadow, he came riding up to Lewallen, smiling.

Lewallen stifled a sigh of annoyance. What did the Comanche want? Lewallen looked past him at Small Buffalo's black pony, which was already grazing in the northern meadow. The animal was small and shaggy and didn't look like much, but Tom Cabral had said he was the fastest of the bunch.

The Indian boy gestured to the black pony and the others he tended, then to the ponies Lewallen had charge of. Then he gestured toward the line of boulders dividing the grazing grounds. He wanted Lewallen to take his string of animals with him, and together they would go to the lower meadow away from the other herders and animals settling down for the day of grazing in the northern pasture.

A broad smile creased Lewallen's face. If they went to the lower meadow, no one in the upper one would see them because of the rock barrier. What a bit of wonderful luck, having the Comanche boy bring the very pony he wanted to the southern pasture. This way he could get the black without anyone knowing it except for this other herder.

But what was he to do with this unexpected and unsuspecting companion, who was unwittingly giving him the advantage that he needed so desperately? Lewallen's brain raced, then suddenly an idea came to him. It would work. It had to work!

Once the two boys and the ponies had passed through the narrow gateway between the two gigantic boulders, Lewallen pointed to the long leather rope the Comanche held and then to one of Many Horses' ponies, a little bay. Next Lewallen made the whirling motion of lassoing it. In a flash the Indian boy had ridden after the bay with his rope twirling. It settled over the pony's neck in one expert try.

"*Tsaa, tsaa!*" Lewallen said admiringly, as he held out his hand for the rope after the Comanche had retrieved it from the bay.

Delighted to show his skill and eager to see what Lewallen could do, the Comanche handed it over.

Whirling the rope as his pa had taught him, Lewallen rode his dun pony to the grazing black and caught it over the head.

"*Tsaa*," cried the laughing Indian boy, as Lewallen rode up to him, pulling the black along the side of the pony he was riding.

The Comanche pointed smilingly to the black as their mounts stood head to head.

Now! Lewallen, all at once, reached swiftly down, caught the Indian boy by one foot, and toppled him from his roan. He could use the boy's mount, too. Grass Woman had pointed it out to him as one of Yellow Wolf's fastest ponies. Besides, he didn't want anyone pursuing him on such a fleet animal.

Before the astonished boy could cry out an alarm, Lewallen was on top of him. He clamped a hand over the Comanche's mouth, and though the boy kicked and struggled, Lewallen wedged a big wad of meadow grass between his jaws. Then he wound a long rawhide rope around and around him, trussing him tightly, even over his grass-filled mouth. The Comanche ponies, trained not to stampede, looked on mildly for a time at the silent fight and went on with their grazing.

It took only a moment to get the food and water Grass Woman had given him off the dun, drive it off with a slap on the rump to graze with the others, put the provisions onto the saddled-and-bridled roan, and mount up.

Then, at a gallop, Lewallen Collier left the meadow with the black pony running on his rope, neck and neck with the roan. Two horses were a danged sight better than one. He not only had one swift animal but two—one to ride, the other to hold in reserve. Lewallen was as well mounted as any Comanche pursuer could be and pounds lighter. If he had any luck at all, it might be noon by the time one of the herders found the gagged boy. And it would take time to get a message to the winter camp to alert the trackers.

But now he had to ride. God above, how he must ride. He needed every second of his head start.

He raced on Yellow Wolf's roan until the pony's sides were heaving, and then before he became lathered Lewallen reined him in. He dismounted and put the roan's bridle into the mouth of the black and mounted it, not taking the precious time to switch the Indian saddle, too. He raced the black over the open prairie before him, putting as many miles between himself and the Comanches as he could. There would be a three-quarter moon that night. He could ride by its light, but sometime during the night he would have to stop to water and rest the ponies.

As Lewallen rode he chose his resting place for the night. It was a spot he'd seen months ago on the way to the buffalo ground, where he'd saved Many Horses' life. It was a wide creek fringed with the usual cottonwoods. At one point, though, the water was overhung by a massive crag of limestone. When he'd first seen the crag, it had struck him as a good hiding place because anything under it was shielded from sight. There'd been a crag a little like it on the banks of the stream near his home.

Lewallen followed his landmarks, always worried that he might lose his way. He took pains to keep the sun on his face, riding east, so he knew he was moving in the right direction. All the same, each time he spied one of the things he'd noticed before, his heart gave a leap. He welcomed with joy each oddly shaped mesquite tree or red-leaf oak, a big pecan tree, a gully opening in the ground in front of him, or a stretch of prairie where many buffalo skulls lay bleached white.

He found the east-west running creek he sought just after moonrise and, mounted for the second time on the black, took the ponies down into the water. While they drank, he ate some of the dried meat from the pouch Grass Woman had given him; then he dismounted into the chill water and led the ponies downstream to the crag. As he waded, he felt coldness for the first time. Though the night wind had been biting, wild excitement and fear had kept him from feeling chilled. But now in the water he suffered from the cold and began to shudder.

Standing in the creek in the sheltered blackness under the crag, Lewallen listened to the sound of the autumn night. There seemed to be nothing but coyotes out tonight. He expected to hear the call of a night bird over the rushing of the stream, but there was nothing. Suddenly Lewallen realized that there were far too many coyotes. They usually hunted alone or in pairs—not in packs like wolves. And this howling was that of a pack.

His heart stopped for an instant. No, not coyotes at all, but Indians signaling each other. Comanches pursuing him! They'd trailed him just as Grass Woman had warned, and they'd made danged good time or they'd found the Comanche boy in the meadow a lot sooner than he expected.

Did they know where he was right now? Or had they only found his tracks before he'd entered the creek? There was no way to know for certain, but he did know that they were there, north of the creek, somewhere above him. As he stood hip deep in the running water he set his mind to working in spite of the cold. And then the idea came to him. It was the kind of harebrained thing Johnny would think up. Although it was dangerous as all get out, still it might work.

Clearly the black pony was the swiftest of the two animals, so he'd use it.

With his foot Lewallen felt for an underwater rock he'd stumbled over, found it, stood up on it, and, shivering with cold and fear, mounted the black once more. As quietly as possible, and leading the roan on a rope, he rode the black pony downstream to the east away from his trackers, praying that the trunks and remaining leaves of the cottonwoods along the creek would shield their silhouettes and that the sound of the running water would cover the small splashing noises he and his ponies made. He went on praying to Heaven that neither pony would start to nicker once they scented the other ponies. Judging from the coyote signals he was hearing, the Comanches were still some distance north of the creek.

Lewallen nudged the black with his knees, urging the pony to go faster through the stream. If the creek grew too deep farther along, the ponies would have to swim. He'd remembered something important now, something that could help him in his escape. There was a burned-out cabin to the east at a fork in the creek. A settler's home had once stood there. He'd wondered about it and the people who'd lived there when he'd ridden by with the Comanches. Lewallen headed now through the water for the cabin and creek fork. Soon the ponies were swimming, and Lewallen let the creek take them along. He went down into the water, holding onto the black's tail and, at the same time, to the neck rope of the roan. Trying not to gasp loudly for air, he arrived at last at the bend where the creek forked.

Lewallen didn't come up out of the creek here. He crawled back up onto the black and reined him over to the shallows, still hauling the roan. He pulled the rope off the roan's neck and headed the pony toward the creek bank with a light kick. The pony didn't need a second kick. He plunged up out of the icy water onto the bank, then started off at a gallop toward the west. The Indians would see his hoof prints and trail him. They might think by the tracks that Lewallen had ridden him out of the creek and had freed the black pony somewhere on the prairie or the black had drowned in the stream. They might be fooled for a time. With luck and courage he might escape yet.

He took the black down into the stream again and, sometimes wading but mostly swimming along its center, rode to the southeast until he found his way blocked by some dead trees across the water.

Lewallen reined in on the eastern bank and listened hard. He'd done what he could to throw the Comanches off his trail. There wasn't one coyote to be heard, but there were night birds about. He didn't think they were Indians calling. He gave the black its head and rode once more to the south and the east, hoping and praying that he'd see more familiar landmarks to guide his way. One thing for sure—there wouldn't be any rest that night for him or for the pony.

Sunrise found him walking the black to save the animal's strength while he ate more of the dried meat. He hadn't sighted any trees or hills that looked familiar since he'd left the creek, but he knew from the stars that had glittered over the prairie that he was going in the right direction to find settlers. Uncle Joshua had been a great one for star lore, and Lewallen blessed the old man's memory for the many hours he'd spent sitting with him and Johnny and Daniel on the steps of the house pointing out the Big Dipper, the North Star, Orion, and the planets.

Midday came and Lewallen, shivering with the cold, stopped at last. Gradually his clothing was drying out. The cold fall wind blowing over the prairie was at a standstill now, too, and he was grateful. As he set the black into a fast pace once more he kept twisting his neck around again and again, looking for Indians and for something, anything, he might remember from before.

He saw no Comanches and no landmarks, but in mid-afternoon he came to something that made him rein in the pony. Marks in the soil! Not the tracks of buffalo but long, narrow, deep, parallel ruts. Wheels had made them. Wagon wheels. The wheel marks continued as far east and west as he could see, but which direction should be taken to find people?

Lewallen made a quick decision and chose to ride east, simply because he knew that there were more folks in East Texas than in West Texas.

After a fast hour's ride east along a river, he sighted

something in the distance rising up out of the prairie. At first he couldn't tell if it was a small, dark bluff or a big rock sticking up out of the ground, but as he approached it his heart jumped. A stockade, by Lord! A settler's palisade of logs that meant someone must have forted up here. Perhaps there were people here right now.

Then to his great joy Lewallen saw the Confederate flag flying over the top of the logs. He shouted at the top of his voice to anyone who might be watching the prairie from the catwalk of the stockade, "Don't shoot! Don't shoot!"

He reined in the pony waiting for a reply, and after a time a deep shout came from the top of the palisade. "Who'd you be?"

"Lewallen Collier from Palo Duro County. Where am I?"

"Fort Belknap, boy. Ride on in."

Lewallen walked Small Buffalo's black pony through a narrow rear gate of the frontier fort. Safe at last, he felt like bawling with relief, but he contained himself. To the first person he saw, a bearded old man in buckskin clothing, he said, "I was a captive of the Comanche Indians till yesterday."

The old man nodded as he closed the heavy gate that had admitted the boy and pony. "You look more like a Comanche than a settler. It was a good thing you yelled so loud. What're you, a half Indian, mebbe?" He glanced up at Lewallen then said, "Nope, I see you got light-colored eyes. Where's your folks?"

Lewallen didn't reply. If he had, the tears would surely have come. Instead he gazed about him at the stone buildings of this fort he'd heard his father mention by name. It was a far distance from the Collier farm, so far no Collier had ever visited it or the tiny frontier town that had sprung up beside it. There were other folks inside here, too, half-grown boys and old men in gray jackets moving about among the buildings. He saw a yellow-haired woman in a blue-calico gown drawing water from a well. She turned to stare at him in curiosity and then went back to her chore.

"What about your folks, boy?" the man repeated.

Swallowing hard first, Lewallen found the words to say, "My pa and brother Johnny rode off to the War. The Indians killed Ma and her uncle and my brother Daniel. All that's left of us is me and Eula Bee."

"Who's that?"

"My little sister. The Comanches took us both away with them, and I escaped." He looked down at the old man. "I got away so's I could find somebody to go back with me and rescue my sister and some other folks from the Comanches. I know where to find their winter camp."

Oddly, instead of getting excited about the news, the old man let out a wheezing sigh. He said, "Get on down now, boy, and go over to that building behind the flagpole while I tend to your horse. Tell the officer in there your story. It's up to him to see what can be done for you, but if you're smart, you won't expect too much."

"What?" Lewallen asked, as he slid down from the pony, feeling suddenly light-headed with weariness.

The old man went on, "I might as well tell you. There's only eleven able-bodied men who could mount up and ride anywhere in here. We ain't the Texas Rangers by a long shot, we ain't. We're the Texas Volunteers, which means we're too old to fight or too young to fight or too stove-up to fight. In all, there ain't no more than twenty folks in the whole danged fort, and six of them are kids and womenfolk. We stay inside the stockade hoping and praying that no Indians come here and no Yankee soldiers either. I suspect you'll be welcome to stay the winter if you've a mind to stay and are willing to earn your keep here."

Lewallen let out a gasp. "Where are the Texas Rangers then?"

"I don't know where they'd be. They ain't here."

Lewallen demanded, "Where does that wagon road go to?"

"Camp Cooper, son. There ain't nobody there at all now. It got mostly burned down after the Yankees moved out of it last February."

Lewallen looked angrily into the old man's faded eyes, then shook his head. Leaving the black pony with him, he hurried to the headquarters building, went up its steps, and beat on the door.

A very young soldier opened the door to the almost bare room that lay beyond it, stared at Lewallen through the thick lenses of his spectacles, then said, "The commanding officer's talking with somebody right now. Just you take a bench over there, and he'll be with you soon as he's done with the man who rode in last week."

"But I have to see him right now!" Lewallen protested. "If we ride straight away to the Comanche camp, maybe we can get there before the men tracing me give up and go back. That'd make fewer Comanches you folks would have to fight."

The soldier's jaw dropped. "Fight? A whole camp of Comanche Indians? Didn't old man Tucker tell you how many of us there are in here?"

"He told me there were eleven of you. With me along that makes twelve, and you got rifles and pistols here, I bet."

The soldier laughed, annoying Lewallen, then said, "I'm sorry. I shouldn't laugh at you. Who'd you be?"

"Lewallen Collier. The Comanches still have my little sister, but I stole a pony and escaped from them."

"I'm gonna sit down beside you here if you don't mind, and you can tell me how you did that. Ain't you worn out, though?"

"Yep, you bet I'm worn out. Even my bones are weary." Lewallen threw a wistful glance at the closed door at the other end of the room, then sat down on the bench with the fair-haired soldier and told him how he'd been captured, of his life with Yellow Wolf's band, of Many Horses, Grass Woman, and Eula Bee, and of how he'd finally gotten away. Now and then the bespectacled soldier would ask him a question in a soft voice. Gradually Lewallen became aware of the deep rumblings of men's voices on the other side of the door.

All at once the voices rose to a shouting that brought Lewallen and the young soldier to their feet with their mouths open. Lewallen put his hand on the soldier's gray coat sleeve to keep him quiet as he listened. He thought he'd heard one of the voices before, and then suddenly he knew who it was. And it didn't delight him one bit.

Lewallen's mouth closed tightly when he saw the door flung open and a tall, long-shanked man come limping out, leaning on a stick for support. There wasn't any mistaking this man, who was gawking at Lewallen as if he'd sprung up out of the mud after a rainstorm.

It was Cabral himself, bearded now and a bit thinner. The leather clothes he'd always worn were a lot dirtier.

The unexpected sight of his old neighbor made Lewallen Collier's tired knees give way, so he sank down on the bench once more.

Tomás had said that he wasn't sure if his father was dead or alive. Well, if seeing was believing, old Cabral was sure enough alive!

SEVEN

Winter

"So you got away from them!" were the first words to burst from Cabral as he stood in the doorway, staring.

At first speechless, Lewallen swallowed hard and managed to say in a harsh, croaking tone, "Your kids, they're alive all right, and so's my sister, Eula Bee. The Comanches still have them, though."

"*Alive? All right?*" Limping, Cabral came over to sit down on the bench and gazed at Lewallen, who could only nod.

"*Dios. Dios!*" were his next words as he let the cane fall to the floor and bent forward with his hands covering his face.

Lewallen looked away from Cabral as a small, fair-haired man in a uniform of Confederate gray came to the door. "Who are you, lad? And what's this about Comanches?" he asked.

"I'm Lewallen Collier from Palo Duro County. I stole a pony and escaped from the Comanches yesterday. Yellow Wolf's Comanches were holding me and my sister and his kids, too." The boy gestured toward Cabral. "I came riding to find help—somebody who'll mount up and go back with me to Yellow Wolf's winter camp."

"I'm Captain Claiborne. We can't help you right now, son. It's my aim to hold the fort against all comers as long as I can with the few men I have. It isn't that we don't care or don't understand about you folks. We just can't go out looking for trouble when we're so outnumbered. Besides, there's womenfolk and children here."

Lewallen flared in anger and surprise. "The Indians killed my ma and little brother and my ma's old uncle."

Captain Claiborne nodded and gestured toward Cabral. "I already know that, son. He told me about his wife and about your folks because he helped bury them all afterward. He came up here hunting for news of his boy and girl."

Lewallen glanced at his old neighbor. "Did you trail us after the Indians attacked?" he asked.

"No. I had two arrows in me and couldn't ride far, so I started out late and by that time the trail was cold."

"Why'd you come here?" Lewallen asked.

"Because folks at forts get news from travelers, and because this fort is in Comanche territory. The minute I saw the Indians at my farm I knew they were Comanches."

"No, sir, you're wrong. Not *every* one of them!" Lewallen shook his head violently. "There was a Kiowa, just one Kiowa, and he's the worst of the bunch. He came with the war party that raided our farm."

"A Kiowa?" Cabral muttered. "I guess that doesn't surprise me much."

Lewallen told him, "Your son Tom's the slave of the Kiowa. Yellow Wolf's got both your daughter and my sister, but they aren't real slaves."

"Yes, that'd be the way of the Comanches," Cabral said quietly.

"All right, come on in, son," the captain told Lewallen. "I want to take down your report like I took Mister Cabral's here, and I'll send it along to Virginia to Army headquarters as soon as a dispatch rider comes through. It's my suggestion to you, seeing that you're alone, that you spend the winter here, and we'll see what we can do come next spring."

"*All winter?*" Lewallen exploded. "What about my sister —and the others?"

Claiborne said heavily, with both hands braced against the sides of the door, "We can only pray that they'll be all right. Now, at least, Mister Cabral knows that his two are still alive."

"Mebbe they won't be, come spring. Winters ain't easy for Indians," he murmured.

"Winters aren't easy for anybody in this part of the world. A norther can come along at any time. One of those storms is another good reason not to take my men out to hunt a winter Comanche camp." Claiborne's voice hardened. "Cabral, I'm tired of arguing with you about a few soldiers wandering over Texas looking for Indians that stole your kids. Now you know who's got them and that they're all right and that this boy claims to know where they are, so that ought to comfort you. But none of this has changed my way of thinking. I am still not riding out to fight Comanches and lose almost all of my men and most likely not get the captives back either. Take your pick. Bide the winter here, or ride out wherever you want this very minute."

"I'll make up my mind what I'm going to do soon as I talk with the Collier boy."

"That's fine by me, Cabral," said the captain, "just as long as you stop bedeviling me and the rest of my men about your family." He turned to the young soldier. "Get some hot coffee and beef and beans from my wife for this boy, and ask her to make up the spare room for him." He crooked a finger at Lewallen. "Come on in now, and don't you worry about your pony. We'll take good care of it."

An hour later, fed and full of coffee but heavy-lidded with fatigue, Lewallen walked across the windswept parade ground, guided by the young soldier. Lewallen had noticed that Cabral wasn't in the headquarters building when he came out of Claiborne's office, so he asked the soldier, "Where does Cabral stay?"

"He's bunking in a building nobody else sleeps in. It's next door to the stables. Nobody wants to be around him since he's so ornery in nature."

"Tell me," Lewallen asked, "did Cabral come riding here on a big, black, wicked-looking horse?"

The soldier nodded as they started together up the walk. "He sure did. He was a mean-looking man on a mean-looking brute, and he brought along two ornery-looking pack mules."

"What did you find out about Cabral here? Did he tell you folks anything about himself?"

"Nope, not to me, he didn't. But I heard the captain tell the sergeant that he knew something about Cabral that sure would make the men at the fort want to take care of him. It had to be something pretty bad, because some of the soldiers we got here ain't exactly been lilies of the field."

Lewallen paused on the veranda, steadying himself against a porch post. He yawned, then asked the soldier, "Do you think Cabral's going to stay the winter here?"

"Yep, I do. Them two arrow wounds'll keep him here if bad weather won't. And besides, now that he knows his kids are all right, he's got more cause to rest up here and get better. All the same the captain's gonna watch him like an owl watches a fat prairie dog while he's here at the fort." The soldier asked suddenly, "Will you be staying or going, Lewallen?"

"I reckon I'll stay," Lewallen answered. "There ain't no reason for me to go back home when they've all gone away or been killed and the cabin's burned down." He smiled wearily. "Besides, the only neighbor us Colliers ever had— even if he wasn't what you'd call a good one—is right here in this fort. It appears to me that Cabral and me have got the same business now."

Without being aware of it, Lewallen Collier slept around the clock in the first true bed he'd crawled into for months. He didn't see the door to the room being opened several times by Mrs. Claiborne, the woman who'd been drawing water from the well when he'd ridden in.

When he awoke, he was startled at first to see the patchwork quilt over him and a curtained window letting in gray light. The room smelled of spices and flowers from a potpourri jar, instead of the eye-biting smoke of the lodge.

Then Lewallen spied the red-calico shirt and gray-cloth trousers lying across the end of the bed. The leather shirt Grass Woman had sewed for him and the tattered pants his ma had made were gone. Underneath the shirt he found socks and long flannel underwear, and a pair of boots were set beside the bed. Whose clothes were these? he wondered. Well, whomever they belonged to, it seemed to him that the Claibornes wanted him to stay awhile.

As he washed his face and hands in the water basin on the bureau, he thought about his future at the fort. What would Captain Claiborne set him to doing to earn his keep? And when would he have that talk with Cabral?

He'd talk with Tom's pa and tell him whatever he could. Maybe Cabral would know something to help both of them get their families back.

Lewallen sighed at his long-haired reflection, thinking he looked more like a Comanche than a Collier. "I've got to keep my temper with Cabral," he said to himself. "After all, he helped bury Ma and Daniel and Uncle Josh. I owe him something for that."

The Claibornes, whose two sons were back East fighting in the War, went out of their way to be nice to Lewallen that first day in their home. They'd given him the cast-off clothing of their younger son, and Mrs. Claiborne stuffed him with biscuits and eggs, fried ham, and grits with milk, the best grub he'd had since his last supper at home.

Mrs. Claiborne spoke with him after that first breakfast. "My husband has told me of what you went through with the Indians, Lewallen. It must have been a dreadful experience for you, simply dreadful. But try to put it out of your thoughts so you can concentrate on your school lessons."

"School?" Lewallen had exploded. "What school?" He hadn't seen any schoolhouse yesterday.

"There isn't any building, Lewallen. I teach the children right here in my parlor. You see, I used to be a teacher back in East Texas where we were stationed."

Lewallen asked her, "Is that why your husband wants me to stay here all winter? Is that why you're being so pleasant to me—so I'll go to school?"

"Of course not, Lewallen. But we believe that as long as you are here with us, you should go to school with the sergeant's children. Can you read and write and figure numbers?"

"I can—some." Lewallen sat back, stifling a groan. His ma had taught him the alphabet and counting and had got him through the first McGuffey Reader. Then she'd gotten too busy tending to Daniel and Eula Bee to teach him more, not that he'd taken much to her lessons to begin with. Mrs. Claiborne was going to get a bad disappointment if she expected him to be good at reading and arithmetic.

Mrs. Claiborne smiled. "A boy with your sand in his craw should have schooling, Lewallen, so he can make his mark in the world. Don't you want to better yourself, Lewallen?"

"Well, ma'am, I thought I was doing all right."

Her soft voice cut him to the core. "You have to take care of your sister if you can get her back, remember? Perhaps you won't want to be a farmer anymore, not when your cabin has been burned down and your stock driven off by the Indians."

"Pa and Johnny will be back soon."

"Soon? I wouldn't rely on that, Lewallen. The Civil War may go on much longer than people think right now. It may even last for years, and many men may be killed and wounded in the fighting."

Lewallen mumbled, "Not Pa. Not Johnny." Then, as he took a third biscuit from the plate she passed him, he said, "All right, I'll come to your school if it would please you. But right now if you don't mind, I'd like to go look up Mister Cabral."

"Oh, yes, the New Mexican." The woman pursed her lips and shook her head as she set the biscuit plate down on the table again.

"New Mexican? I thought he was a Mexican—or half Mexican." Lewallen said.

"No, Cabral is a New Mexican, I'm told. Of course, go find the man, Lewallen."

The autumn wind whipping across the parade ground bit into Lewallen's face, making him wince. One glance at the darkening sky showed him that bad weather was on its way. It wouldn't be a norther because the air earlier in the morning hadn't been wet and heavy, but this sky could sure mean snow. Lewallen was grateful that whatever weather was on its way hadn't caught him out on the prairie and that he hadn't waited too long to escape.

He rapped on the door of the shed next to the stables, but nobody answered. So he went to the stables, opened a side door, and stepped inside. For a while he waited, letting his eyes get used to the dim light while he inhaled the warm, sweetish scent of the horses.

"Hey, Mister Cabral!" he called out. "I'm here—Lewallen Collier."

"I seen you from the very first," came a deep voice from behind him.

Lewallen swung about and saw Cabral sitting on a keg top, braiding leather thongs into a hackamore. His green eyes were fixed on him, looking up from under the brim of his big Mexican hat.

He said, "I tended to the black pony you rode here and put horseshoes on him. I stole an Indian pony once when I was your age and rode off with it, too."

Lewallen nodded. "Tom told me. I took two Indian ponies." And then he described how he let the roan go free to deceive the trackers.

"Think you're pretty smart, don't ya, Collier? How come my Tom didn't bust loose from the camp, too?"

"Because the Kiowa, Small Buffalo, didn't set Tom to guarding ponies."

"I reckon that makes some sense to me. You say that Yellow Wolf's the head chief?"

"That's right."

Cabral grunted. "As I figure it, Yellow Wolf ought to be about fifty years old."

"Yep, I guess so. Do you know Yellow Wolf?"

"I used to."

"Do you know Many Horses, too?"

"No, not Many Horses."

"Were you a prisoner of the Comanches, too?"

"Nope, not them. The Utes. Sit down and tell me. Where's Yellow Wolf's camp now?"

Lewallen found another keg, rolled it over near Cabral's, upended it, and sat down between two rows of horses switching their tails and eating oats from mangers. As best he could, he told Cabral of the canyon location of the Comanche winter camp.

When he finished, Cabral said, "I know the place. I could find it if I wanted to, but there ain't much point trying to get there in the bad weather that's coming. It'd be different if you'd rode in a week earlier."

Stung, Lewallen said, "I ran away the first chance I got. What do you think I should've done, stay there till spring? If I had, you wouldn't have heard that your kids were all right."

"That's true enough. I reckon I'm glad I didn't shoot you that day down by the creek."

Lewallen muttered, "Thanks, I guess. Well, what do you aim to do about Tom and Angelita, seeing as how you know Yellow Wolf?"

"Go after them as soon as I can before the Comanches break up their winter camp and move on. These chicken-hearted soldiers won't ever go out after them, so I'll go ransom my two kids myself."

"Ransom? What does that mean?"

"Buy them back with the goods I got on my pack mules. I sold my farm and put most of the money into buying things Indians like. I planned to wander among the Comanche bands searching for my kids if the Army wouldn't look for them. Maybe Yellow Wolf will sell my kids back to me if I give him enough trade goods."

Ransom! The new word seared itself into Lewallen's mind. He didn't have a single thing to buy Eula Bee back with. He asked Cabral, "What about my sister?"

"What've you got to buy her back with?"

"Nothing but the clothes I rode in here wearing and the black pony."

"The one that belonged to the Kiowa?"

"Yes. The black's his best racer."

"Well then, he'll sure be wanting it back, but it don't appear to me that you can take the pony back there to him yourself."

"No, I don't think I can." Lewallen fell silent. "I wanted the Confederate Army to get Eula Bee back."

"Not the soldiers here, Collier. It'd cost them lives. Nope, as I see it, I got to do this alone."

"No, you don't Cabral, not alone! My sister's there, too, remember!" Lewallen jumped to his feet, startling the horse behind him so that she lashed out with a rear foot, narrowly missing him.

Cabral offended Lewallen by chuckling. "What do you want me to do—ride into the camp with a runaway slave on a stolen pony? I've hung on to my hair a long time now, and I plan to keep it."

Lewallen cried out, "If you know Yellow Wolf, how come the Comanches raided your farm?"

"Because none of the warriors knew me."

In desperation Lewallen asked, "Take me with you when you go. My pa told me to look after Eula Bee."

"I don't need you, boy," were Cabral's hard words. Then he added, "As I see it, I could do better alone."

Lewallen replied with the first thing that darted into his mind. "I know where the winter camp is, and I know something more. I know where the Comanches plan to go in the springtime." He didn't know, but would Cabral believe that he did? Cabral knew the ways of the Comanches as well as he did.

Cabral asked calmly, "Now where would that be, I wonder, south or east of the canyon?"

"I ain't going to tell you where it is—not unless you promise to take me with you."

Lewallen turned around and stalked out of the stable. Let Cabral think about what he'd said. He wasn't going to stick around and let the man try to wheedle him into revealing that he was only bluffing.

EIGHT
Time to Go

That same evening, after supper, Lewallen told the Claibornes of his conversation with Cabral.

The captain was silent for a time, then said, "Well, he's a queer cuss and worse company. Maybe you'd be wisest, Lewallen, to let him go off by himself if that's what he wants. Let him ransom your sister and fetch her back here. It's lonely here. My wife and I wouldn't mind having a little girl around the place, you know."

Lewallen said bitterly, "He can't do that. I haven't got anything to ransom her with, even if I trusted Cabral to do the job."

"Have you thought about selling the Comanche pony?" asked Claiborne.

"But how can I sell it if I'm gonna be stuck here all winter?"

"I'll buy it. You said the black's a good racer, didn't you?"

"Yes, but it's an Indian horse."

"No matter," said Claiborne. "I hope to be transferred from here sometime next year, and we'll take the black along with us. Indian ponies have often been known to beat out blooded horses in races."

105

Mrs. Claiborne let out a long deep sigh and got up from the table. "Gambling," Lewallen heard her mutter disgustedly.

Lewallen nodded at the captain, then asked. "What'll you give me for the pony?"

"Fifty dollars, and that's being generous."

Lewallen looked directly into Captain Claiborne's face and said, "Fifty dollars and a horse and gear. I'll buy trade goods and supplies out of the money to ransom my sister with, but I have to have a good horse for the journey, so I can trail along with Cabral when he goes after his kids." Lewallen's forehead clouded with concern, even though he could see that Claiborne would agree to the new bargaining terms. "I'm worried, sir, that Cabral will sneak out some night without me and go off looking for the Comanche camp all on his own."

"He won't be doing that, lad," came a flat statement from Claiborne. "There are men posted on the catwalks of the stockade twenty-four hours a day. No one gets out of here without first getting my permission to leave. Cabral will get himself shot before he reaches any one of the gates. That goes for you, too, Lewallen, and everyone else."

A sigh of relief passed Lewallen's lips. Then he said, "Cabral claims that he knows the peace chief, Yellow Wolf."

Claiborne sipped from his cup and said, "That's the last of our coffee now that the War's finally come."

Lewallen stifled a sigh. Apparently the Claibornes weren't about to talk to him about Cabral and the Comanches. He tried again, "I hear that Cabral knows a lot about Indians. He says he was a captive of the Ute tribe when he was a boy. Ain't the Utes in New Mexico Territory?"

"That's where they were last time I heard," agreed Captain Claiborne.

Lewallen said, trying once more for information, "I bet Cabral knows the Indian sign language and maybe Comanche, too, if he knows Yellow Wolf."

"Well, son," Claiborne answered, "many white men know sign language. And the most common Indian language on the plains is Comanche. Lots of people speak it."

"All this talk of Indians is interesting to you two but not to me," Mrs. Claiborne put in suddenly. She reached out and touched Lewallen on the arm. "I hope you won't take it amiss if I cut your hair before it gets so long you'll have to braid it in two Indian-style braids."

"Two braids—that's the Comanche way, ma'am. You ought to see how a Kiowa man braids his. It's something." Lewallen's face darkened, thinking of Small Buffalo.

" I don't want to see a Kiowa. I want you to look like the Texas boy you are. After cutting your hair, I want to see how well you can read."

Lewallen shuffled his feet under the table, embarrassed. This Mrs. Claiborne was the sort of lady a person said "ma'am" to without being ordered to, and Captain Claiborne was a "sir" for sure. He'd see that old Cabral didn't get out of the fort without his knowing it.

But he wouldn't tell the Claibornes everything he and Cabral had talked about. They wouldn't approve of his lying about knowing where the Comanches would set up their spring camp.

Instead he told Mrs. Claiborne, "All right, ma'am, I'll read for you, though I don't think it's going to please you hearing me fall all over the words. Thank you kindly for being so good to me here. It would please my ma to know there were such good folks in this part of Texas."

Winter struck the fort in earnest the next day with a heavy fall of snow. Afterward came piercing, cold winds that made the sentries on the catwalks complain bitterly.

For Lewallen Collier, however, that winter of 1861 was a snug and comfortable one except for his school lessons with Mrs. Claiborne and the other children. He didn't like the penmanship and spelling, and he found the reading lessons barely tolerable, although by February he was confessing to himself that a partiality to arithmetic was creeping up on him. Arithmetic was mighty neat in its ways, something a man could put his trust in because it didn't slip and slide around the danged way spelling words did.

He had only two more conversations with Cabral, and each time he had to seek the man in the stables. The first talk was early in December, when he told Cabral that he'd sold Small Buffalo's pony and got cash to buy trade goods at the sutler's store in the fort and that Claiborne had thrown a blue-roan horse and gear into the deal. Cabral didn't say a word to Lewallen, only grunted and went about his business, currying his big black horse.

The second time Lewallen sought him out was to tell him that he'd bought thirty-five-dollars' worth of glass beads and beading needles to please Yellow Wolf and his wives so they'd be willing to give up Eula Bee. He said, "I would've bought blankets, but beads are easier to carry when I have only one horse. What do you think of my getting beads, Mister Cabral?"

"Why ask me, Collier? You lived with the Comanches. You ought to know what they want."

Lewallen ignored this remark and asked, "What're you taking along?"

"A number of things." And Cabral turned away, limping down the line of horses to his big black's stall.

The winter went by slowly while Lewallen stayed with the hospitable Claibornes. He missed Johnny and his pa and wished there was some way to hear from them before he went out after Eula Bee, but most of all he found that he missed his mother and Daniel. At night in the dark, he gave himself at last to weeping for them. After his tears were done, he'd lie back staring into the blackness, thinking of Eula Bee in the Comanche camp, wondering if she was possibly thinking of him, too. He was certain that Tom Cabral had gotten word to her that her brother planned to come back for her as soon as he could. It was too danged bad that Tom couldn't whistle "Lorena," to remind her of her life with her family.

Spring came at last with rains that rapidly melted the snow and made a torrent of the river that ran near the stockade of the fort.

One Saturday morning, after he'd climbed the ladder to the catwalk to look out onto a prairie that showed only patches of snow, Lewallen decided in his mind that it was time. Time to go. The warm winds of April touched his face, and in their scent was something that fed an itching restlessness and a longing for the sight of his sister.

Maybe Cabral was feeling the same way about his kids. Lewallen walked to the stables, opened a door, and went inside quietly, so as not to startle the horses in their stalls. He called out, "It's me, Cabral, Lewallen Collier. I come to ask when you plan to leave here."

The deep voice came in reply, "Come on in and see for yourself, kid."

Lewallen walked into the long stables to an open space used for saddling. There he found Cabral cinching up the saddle of his big black horse. The packs of the two mules were already loaded, and the animals were wearing halters.

Lewallen demanded, "Have you got permission to go?"

"Yep, just ten minutes past."

"You weren't going to wait for me!" the boy accused angrily. Then he flared, "Well, I'm going, too. I'll saddle up and ride out after you. I'll catch up."

Lewallen didn't wait for Cabral to say anything. He spun around and ran through the stables and outside, sprinting for the Claiborne quarters. He flung open the kitchen door, ran past Mrs. Claiborne, who was kneading dough for bread, and into the spare room, where he rolled up a bedroll of blankets she had told him he could have. Then he took the leather sacks of trade beads out of the bedroom chest and went back through the house to the kitchen, where Mrs. Claiborne stood.

He asked her, "Please, ma'am, Cabral's going out today. Could you fix me a bag of food for the trip?"

She looked up. "Lewallen, are you sure you want to go?"

"Yes, ma'am, I am. He's my best chance, as I see it, to get Eula Bee. That's what Ma would have wanted." He hesitated, then asked, "Wouldn't one of your sons have done the same thing for his baby sister if he knew you wanted him to?"

She took her hands out of the dough and wiped them off with a towel. Then she said with a sigh, "God bless you, Lewallen. All right, go on. I'll come to the stables in a few minutes with the food."

"I'll need permission from the captain."

"Yes, of course."

Lewallen ran back to the stables to the stall of the horse Captain Claiborne had given him as part of their trade. He led the gelding out, put the bridle into his mouth, and threw on the saddle. Then he waited, asking himself how he was going to say good-bye and thank-you to Mrs. Claiborne and her husband.

When she came to the stable, Captain Claiborne was with her. They each carried a saddlebag of provisions. They stood beside Lewallen and his roan, as Cabral led his black horse and the pack mules past them out of the stable. He didn't glance at them, and they didn't bid him farewell.

After Cabral had gone, Mrs. Claiborne said, "Lewallen, I wish you weren't going off with that man. I'm pleased he's leaving the fort, but I wish you weren't traveling with him."

"Ma'am, like I told you, he's my best chance of getting Eula Bee back. I don't truly think I could do it alone."

Captain Claiborne said softly, "Lewallen, I could call the guard and hold you here by force."

"I'm asking you not to do that, please. Eula Bee ought to be waiting and watching for me now that spring's come."

"All right, Lewallen, go. But remember, please, you will have a home with us whenever you like until your father comes back to Texas."

"I'll hold that in mind. Thank you kindly for all you've done for me. I wish I could say I'd done as much for you."

Mrs. Claiborne told him, "You've brightened the winter for all of us, Lewallen. It would have been a hard Christmas for us without having a boy in the house."

"Give her a hug," came from the captain.

Bright red with blushing, Lewallen let Mrs. Claiborne come forward and embrace him and kiss him on the cheek. She smelled good, of rose water and spices, as she said, "Good-bye and good luck. I'll pray for you and your sister." She whirled about and left hurriedly, her nose buried in a handkerchief.

"Good-bye, son," came from the captain. "I'll go out and see that the sentries let you go after Cabral."

Alone now, Lewallen swallowed hard, grabbed the reins of his horse, and led it outside, where he mounted up in the pale sunlight.

Three minutes later he was riding out of the fort through the side gate, which was being held open for him by the same old soldier who'd let him in last autumn.

"Good luck, sprout," were the soldier's words.

"Thank you."

Lewallen's eyes weren't on him, though, but fixed on the prairie ahead where he could see Cabral and his pack mules going northward.

He clicked his tongue to the blue roan, nudged him with his knees, and sent him into a canter that would soon catch up to Cabral. He didn't expect any warm welcome from him, but he didn't expect him to try to drive him off either, not with the eyes of the soldiers still on them. And there might be another reason—that Cabral believed Lewallen's story that he knew where to find Yellow Wolf's spring camp.

When Lewallen drew up to ride beside Cabral, he gave Lewallen a strange look out of the corner of one greenish eye and went on riding in silence.

Lewallen told him, "We don't want to ride due north, mister. We want to go mostly west right now. That's where we'll find the Indians."

"All right. Suit yourself, Collier. You lead the way."

"Nope, we ride side by side from now on, Mister Cabral." He'd decided to call him mister instead of sir.

"Do you think I aim to put a bullet into your back, boy?"

"No, there wouldn't be much point in your doing that or in my shooting you if I had a pistol." Lewallen eyed the man's rifle in its saddle holster and the pistol at his right hip. "It's just that it's more equallike for us to ride side by side, seeing that we're both on the same errand."

He heard Cabral laugh, then saw him rein his horse's head toward the west. Afterward, except for the sound of the wind and clinking of horse gear, there was silence. As they rode Lewallen worried about the exact whereabouts of the Comanches.

In the end he decided to take Cabral to the winter camp in the hopes that the Indians hadn't left it yet. It was in high country, where there would probably be a good deal more snow than on the prairie. They could still be there.

❋ ❋ ❋

Lewallen wondered who'd be the cook when they made camp. As it turned out, Cabral tended to the work without even suggesting Lewallen do it. He stirred up a tasty dish of onions, bacon, biscuits, water, and dried meat that astonished Lewallen with its flavor.

"You must have been on the trail a lot, Mister Cabral," he said. "You sure can cook."

"I done my share of camp chores, all right, boy," was his only comment.

"Mister Cabral, do you think Many Horses is going to try to kill me when I come back? I saved his life, you know."

"Did you? No, you never got around to telling me that. What happened?" Cabral was looking at Lewallen over the rim of his tin mug with true interest.

"Hunting buffalo." Then he told Cabral the story.

Cabral said afterward, "I reckon Many Horses more than likely won't kill you, though he might want to keep you as his slave again. As I see it, he owes you your life."

"I could try to buy myself from him with my beads, the way I plan to buy Eula Bee."

Cabral laughed as he set down his mug beside the fire. "I don't think that'd suit him. What's to stop him from keeping you and the beads both, kid?"

"*You*, Mister Cabral."

"*Me?* You got plenty of brass, as well as grit, Collier. Why should I take on your troubles, too?"

Lewallen took a deep breath. "Mister Cabral, I want to get my sister back. I think you owe it to me to help me out however you can. First of all, you owe me something for telling you about Tom and Angelita."

"Collier, I would've heard that back at the fort anyhow. You didn't come to the fort to tell me that—but to get soldiers."

"There's more that you owe me for."

"Now what would that be?"

"For not fighting Tom with a knife when the Indians wanted me to."

Cabral nodded. How ugly he was with the firelight on his long, seamed face! "All right, tell me about it. Why didn't you fight him? You never acted so damned fond of Tomás before."

"Because Daniel was his friend and because I'm a lot bigger than Tom. And because that's what the Comanches wanted, and Tom warned me to be brave. So instead I went after the Kiowa with the knife they gave me."

Cabral's glance was sharp and searching. He shook his head, then said, "All right, I do owe you. I'll make an offer to Many Horses to ransom you."

"What about my sister, Eula Bee? I'll give you beads for her, too."

"All right, her, too. But you better pray that Many Horses will take what's offered to him. The People can drive a sharp bargain when they want to."

"Thank you, Mister Cabral." Lewallen looked at his well-cleaned plate. He said, embarrassed, staring at its surface, "When I escaped from the winter camp, I knew that I was sorry that I hadn't been a friend to Tom the way Daniel was. Eula Bee and Angelita are still friends. They've got each other now. Tom's the worst off, being the slave of Small Buffalo."

"I can see you don't take to him."

"Let me tell you why. You don't know everything." Lewallen told of the actions of the Kiowa brave at his farm and finished by saying, "You bet I don't like him! He's got the scalps of my family on his lance, and he was sure after mine, too. Most of all, I hate his having my ma's scalp. Nobody ought to do that to womenfolk."

Sitting cross-legged, Cabral grunted, then said, "Lots of white men don't hold back when it comes to killing Indians. Any Indian—man, woman, or papoose—is the same to them. It's a thing for you to bear in mind, Collier."

"Mister Cabral, that's what Grass Woman told me, and she wasn't a Comanche but a white woman." Suddenly emboldened by the first friendliness he'd seen from his old neighbor, Lewallen asked, "How come you know some of the Comanche men when it was the Utes you lived with?"

"Because I was a Comanchero, until I came here to Texas to settle down."

"What's a Comanchero?"

"A New Mexican who trades with the Comanches— selling whatever the Indians want to buy. It ain't a trade that makes a man exactly popular with Texas folks these days."

So this was what Captain Claiborne had known about Cabral and had kept secret from the men at the fort!

Lewallen asked, "What're you doing here in Texas then?"

"Staying out of New Mexico Territory. I got in a fight

there with a saloonkeeper and killed him." Cabral grinned at Lewallen. "You see Texas men who get themselves into trouble with the law go to New Mexico Territory and change their names. You could say I done it the other way around, pardner."

"Pardner?" Lewallen caught at the word. Partner to a Comanche trader? No wonder Cabral, if that was his real name, knew Yellow Wolf. But Cabral must have done his Indian trading some years ago since he didn't know the younger warrior, Many Horses. Sure, Cabral as an old acquaintance could surely handle the ransoming with the Comanches. Come to think about it, that's why Tom had been surprised that the Indians attacked their home. Tom had known about his pa's past work, but had probably not known the name his pa used in New Mexico Territory. So when Tom complained to the Indians about attacking the Cabral farm, they hadn't understood him.

Lewallen understood a number of things now. He could see why Cabral hadn't been so pleased to have him tag along. He could be a source of trouble. In letting him come, Cabral was truly trying to repay Lewallen's kindness to his son.

Lewallen asked, "Is that why you folks were so unfriendly to us when we were neighbors?"

"That was part of it. We didn't want you or anybody else to get too close to us. The other part was that I didn't like being thought of as a greaser, a Mexican, by your pa and ma. I'm not a Mexican, but my wife was, and I wasn't going to let nobody insult her to her face."

Ashamed and wanting to make some sort of amends for

himself, Lewallen said, "She was a mighty pretty little lady as I remember. Angelita takes after her, I reckon."

"Yes, she does. My Angelita does look like her mother, and I want to have her back."

"I surely do hope you get her back, Mister Cabral—pardner."

NINE

Ransom

Retracing his cross-country escape turned out to be more difficult than Lewallen had expected. Trees that had been landmarks earlier looked somehow different in shape and foliage, and in some places snow still lay on the ground. To add to his bafflement, there were large numbers of new, tiny lakes that Cabral told him would dry up by summer, but now their unexpected presence confused him. And traveling was slowed down in spring because the rivers were swollen.

The ruins of the settler's house beside the stream he had swum down had withstood the high waters of the creek, however. There Lewallen told Cabral he was sure of his bearings. They had reached the place where he had set the roan free. Cabral smiled, then nodded his head, letting Lewallen know that he was impressed by his trick.

Since their talk around the campfire that first night away from the fort, Cabral had become more friendly, but as Lewallen's pa would have put it, "He ain't the sort to fall all over a person."

Cabral said at the ruins, "It's my guess, though, that the Comanches split up here. Some of them were still on your trail and expected to stay on it till you came up to that wagon road that went to the fort."

"More than likely, but I didn't see any of them."

Cabral nodded again, then surprised Lewallen with a question. "You don't truly know where Yellow Wolf's gone to now that it's springtime, do you, Collier?"

"Nope, not truly, I guess I don't." Caught in his lie, Lewallen couldn't meet Cabral's eyes. He looked at his horse's twitching ears and muttered, "but I can take us to the winter camp in the canyon." He glanced up, hoping Cabral wasn't angry with him. No, he didn't seem to be. He wasn't smiling, but he wasn't looking mad either. Lewallen went on, "I only said I knew where they'd be in the spring so you wouldn't leave me behind along the way."

"I believed you at first, kid. But no matter now. I reckon we'll get to the winter camp and find them gone. I'll trail them from there, though, even if it's out of our way and will take time."

"But they might still be in the canyon."

"Nope, it's turning warm too soon this year for that. It wasn't so cold a winter that they'd still be snowed in in the high country. They'll be wanting fresh meat and good grass for their ponies bad by now. More than likely they had sickness in the winter, too."

"Why would that be?" Lewallen's mind surged toward Eula Bee. Would she be sick? He recalled Grass Woman's words that many children died among The People, her own included.

"Indians get sick, too—the young ones in particular. Well, let's get on our way now, Collier."

*   *   *

The winter camp of the Comanches was just as Cabral had predicted—deserted—though there were a number of traces that it had been inhabited. Buffalo hides and lodge covers too worn to be useful anymore had been left behind under the trees, and there were many little, circular, dark pits that had been the fires of the various lodges.

Lewallen and Cabral camped there one night. While Lewallen got their supper for a change on the very spot where he'd dug the fire hole for Grass Woman, Cabral wandered alone about the canyon on foot. He came back before long with a grim expression on his whiskery face.

"There's been sickness this winter. I know the ways of The People, Collier. They don't put their dead up in the air on scaffolds. They put them into holes in the rocks and cliffs and shut up the holes. I've counted five places where that's been done here this winter."

Lewallen felt his heart stop beating for an instant. "Was one of them a kid, do you think, Mister Cabral."

"There ain't no way of knowing just by looking at the outside of a cliff or a heap of rocks. And that's all I plan to do. It don't do to disturb their dead ones."

"Yep, that's right." The Texas boy shuddered, then asked, "We'll be leaving here tomorrow morning?"

"You bet, bright and early, we're leaving."

Lewallen filled the tin plates with beans and fried sowbelly. When he handed Cabral his, he gave him a searching glance. Cabral's long face was mournful as he ate. He was no doubt thinking of Tom and Angelita, as surely as Lewallen was of Eula Bee, wondering how they'd fared through the winter.

❊   ❊   ❊

Joe Cabral never told Lewallen, who was still too wary of his temper to ply him with a lot of idle questions, where he learned to track. But he knew how all right. He taught Lewallen what to look for as they rode eastward over the prairie together—hoof prints near mud puddles, horse and dog droppings, the faint double-line traceries of a dragged travois, marks in grass and fire holes where tepees had been erected, as well as bones of recently killed antelope and deer.

After an inspection of an abandoned campsite by one of the new temporary lakes, Cabral told Lewallen, "They're wandering now, but I think we'll catch up to them soon. Maybe tomorrow or the next day. It won't do to come galloping down on them at nighttime."

"Nope, it surely wouldn't." Lewallen asked anxiously, "You haven't spotted more burying places, have you?"

With his back to him Cabral shook his head as he checked one of the saddlebags of his smaller pack mule.

Three days later, in midafternoon, they found the Comanches stopped beside a creek, whose swirling waters carried so much mud that it was brown. An apprehensive, fearful Lewallen had earlier that day asked Cabral how he intended to approach the Indians and been told in a sharp manner, "Don't you worry your head on that score, pardner. I plan to do it."

"But what about me?"

"You stick to me like I owed you money and let me do all the talking—even if you can figure out what they might be saying to me."

"Yes, I'll do that. But what about Many Horses?"

"I'll dicker with him. The way I see it, he saved you from that Kiowa, and you saved him from the buffalo. That evens matters up. Don't fret now. Keep quiet. Act brave even if you don't feel brave. You know how the Comanches feel about brave folks."

It didn't surprise Lewallen, though it didn't comfort him either, when Cabral lifted his right hand and came riding bold as could be out of a screen of cottonwoods downstream, toward six Comanche braves who were watering their ponies at the water's edge.

Lewallen knew some of the Indians by sight, if not by name, and he saw how they at once readied their bows with arrows, aiming at him and Cabral. Cabral shouted out, "*Haints*," the word Lewallen knew meant "friend." He then gave the reins of the restless pack mules, who scented the Indian ponies, to Lewallen and began to gesture rapidly with his hands as he spoke. He pointed repeatedly to the pack mules.

For quite a while Cabral was the only one to speak, then one of the Comanches replied to him in sign language. Finally the Indians put their weapons away and went on watering their ponies, ignoring Lewallen and Cabral, who waited. Afterward the braves mounted and rode up to them, staring again and again from Lewallen's face to Cabral's, while one of them spoke with Cabral.

"Sing your song, Collier," ordered Cabral. "They told me just now what they call you and that you belong to Many Horses. Don't worry. We ain't going directly to him; our important business is with Yellow Wolf."

Because his throat had gone dry from tension, Lewallen began whistling, not singing, "Lorena," telling himself it would let Eula Bee and Tomás know, and perhaps Angelita, too, that he'd come back as he'd promised.

Escorted by watchful and silent warriors, Lewallen and his old neighbor rode through the camp, which the women were still in the process of setting up. Dogs followed, snapping at the heels of the horses, and were whipped away by children and old people, who stared curiously after the riders as they passed.

Although Lewallen's eyes searched everywhere, he wasn't rewarded by the sight of his little sister. Nor did he see either of the Cabrals. He saw Grass Woman, though, and Holds the Arrows, who paused in their work of erecting a lodge to gape at him. He saw Grass Woman shake her head as if to tell him he should never have returned. This one gesture warned him of her husband's probable feelings toward his former slave boy. Lewallen nudged his horse closer to Cabral's, shouldering the smaller Indian ponies out of his way with ease.

He asked Cabral anxiously, "Did they say that Many Horses is in the camp today?"

Cabral didn't answer but spoke to the Comanche riding on his left.

Lewallen caught the Indian's word, "*Kee*." "No." Then he heard something about "hunting." Many Horses was on a hunting party. That was good news for sure. Lewallen sang out "Lorena" as loudly as he could, trying to keep his voice from breaking with nervousness.

As Yellow Wolf came out of his painted lodge to greet

Cabral and Lewallen the boy stopped singing. For a panic-stricken instant he relived that fearful moment when he'd first set eyes on the chief.

Cabral lifted his hand and spoke at length to Yellow Wolf in Comanche and in sign language. He kept saying one word over and over, *"Haints, haints,"* the same word Many Horses had used when he'd saved him from the buffalo herd.

At last the peace chief echoed the word, *"Haints"* and approached Cabral. Ignoring Lewallen, he took Cabral's hand and shook it. Then Yellow Wolf pointed to Lewallen, frowned deeply, and spoke in rapid Comanche, his dark gaze constantly on the boy.

In spite of the chilly spring wind Lewallen began to perspire. He guessed the drift of the conversation. It was about his stealing two ponies, one of them Yellow Wolf's, and escaping when Many Horses had trusted him.

What was Cabral saying to get him out of this deep trouble?

Finally Cabral turned his head and told Lewallen in a low tone, "They found the roan. Yellow Wolf say he thinks Small Buffalo, his son-in-law, would sell the black pony for a pound of your best trade beads. I told him I brought beads and beading needles with me, too. I guess the matter of the two ponies you took could be settled easy enough. That went smooth for you, Collier, but I ain't doing so well for myself. Small Buffalo rode away some time ago, back to the Kiowa band he belongs to. He took my boy Tomás with him." Cabral shook his head warningly. "Keep quiet now while I ask some more questions. Yellow Wolf is glad to see me but not you, a pony stealer. He expects me to give him something for welcoming me, and I plan to do that. Then I'll ask him what he wants for ransoming my daughter."

Lewallen asked, "When you ask about Angelita, ask him about Eula Bee, too."

"Kid, I told you to keep quiet."

Cabral dismounted and went to one of the pack mules. He opened a saddlebag and took out a blue-and-scarlet blanket, which he gave to Yellow Wolf. After more talk he gave the beaming Comanche a long string of white, glistening, seashell beads, which made the Indians gathered about gasp in admiration.

While Cabral was giving a second string of shell beads to Yellow Wolf, Lewallen's gaze swept again and again over the gathered crowd of Indians, searching in vain for his sister's red head or for Angelita.

Cabral went on talking and gesturing with the peace chief but stopped suddenly. Not only had he fallen silent, he seemed to be sagging against the pack animal, clutching at his hip as if his old arrow wounds were about to make him fall down.

After a time Cabral lifted his head to stare into Lewallen's face. His look was tragic. He said dully, "She's dead. Died last winter."

"*Dead?*" The horrible word dug knifelike into Lewallen's heart. Eula Bee dead? In spite of his resolve to show no fright a long groan escaped him. No wonder he hadn't been able to find his sister among the crowd of curious Indians.

As his eyes met Cabral's and saw their glaze of misery, he sensed all at once that he was mourning his own child—not Eula Bee!

"*Angelita?*" whispered Lewallen.

"That's what Yellow Wolf just told me. She died of lung fever the same month Snow Moon's baby girl was born dead. He has mourned them both."

"*Eula Bee?* Did you ask about her?" Lewallen asked hoarsely.

"Not yet, let me ask the chief about her next. You be quiet now."

In an agony Lewallen listened to the long talk of the Comanchero and the peace chief. It seemed to him that they would never stop speaking.

At last a sunken-eyed Cabral, whose cheeks seemed carved now into even deeper lines above his sprouting, graying beard, looked up at the boy and said in a flat, hard voice. "You're in luck again. Your sister ain't dead. She's gone away, though. Yellow Wolf says a chief of another band, somebody more important than he is, spent the winter in the canyon with them. One of that chief's wives took a big shine to your sister. Yellow Wolf got in a gambling game with the other chief and lost ten ponies and, along with them, your sister. She went off with the other chief the day they busted up the winter camp."

"Where'd they go?"

"I asked him. He don't know. Them other Comanches generally roam way north of Yellow Wolf's band—up on the Staked Plains. He supposes they went back up there."

"*Eula Bee!*" the name burst out of Lewallen in a soft wail.

"Shut your mouth. Don't make noises like a coyote," Cabral told him brutally. "She's alive, ain't she? That's more than I can say about Angelita. Now I got to ask some more about Small Buffalo and about what Many Horses will want as ransom for you, so I can get both of us out of here alive."

"But Many Horses ain't in the camp now."

"He ain't here, no, but plenty of his friends are. I aim to get away from here fast as I can now. According to Yellow Wolf, them beads of yours will settle things with Small Buffalo for the black pony, but I still have to ransom you."

"I'll do it myself—with the beads."

"Shut up. You wait! Let me talk some more to the chief, but get out some beads just in case."

Lewallen took his feet out of the stirrups and slid to the ground to open one of his saddlebags packed with the small sacks of beads he'd gotten at the fort. All at once he realized that a familiar voice was whispering in English. Grass Woman! She'd come up through the crowd to stand directly behind him and speak into his ear.

"Lewallen, why did you come back?"

"To get my sister. What other reason would I have?"

"She's left the camp."

"I know. Grass Woman, do you think Many Horses will give me up for a pound of embroidery beads and some needles?"

"My husband valued you, Lewallen."

Lewallen sighed. "I sort of valued him, too, but I ain't a Comanche like you. What'll he want to let me go?"

"A blanket and beads, though they will make his heart heavy. He thought of you as a friend, perhaps someday a son."

"No, ma'am, I'm sorry, but I would never be a son to him or to you either. I just could never feel right about it when my family was killed by Comanches. And I still have a real pa." Without looking at her, Lewallen called to Cabral, "Many Horses' wife talks English. She says she thinks her husband'll take some trade goods as ransom." He turned to face her. "Are you sure a blanket and beads will keep Many Horses from coming after us later on?"

"I believe it will. He has much honor."

Grass Woman was thinner than last autumn, and her blue eyes were very large. They filled with tears as she said, "I'm sorry about the little Mexican girl dying. We did everything we could to save her."

"How was Eula Bee when she left here? Was she sick, too?" Lewallen demanded. Anger was rising now. Here he was buying his freedom when he should never have been among the Indians in the first place. Furthermore, his sister had been lost in a gambling game—like a pony or iron kettle!

"Your sister was well. The winter was hard, but she was fine throughout. How was your winter, Lewallen?"

"Mighty fine. I spent it at a fort where I slept in a bed. Are you sure you don't want to go back to the white people yourself?"

At the expected shaking of her head he turned his back on her, pulled out a canvas poke of tiny multicolored beads, and handed it to her.

When he felt her take it, he buckled the saddlebag again and remounted his horse. Then he said, "Would you give Grass Woman a blanket, too, Mister Cabral? I'll pay you back later."

Lewallen watched Grass Woman go to Cabral, who put a bright red-and-yellow wool blanket over her outstretched arms. Cabral stood watching as she pushed through the throng toward Lewallen again; then he started to speak once more with Yellow Wolf.

Grass Woman paused beside Lewallen's horse, looking up at him. She said, "He is a clever man, this Comanchero. I have heard tales of him from the old women of the band. If Many Horses had known this Comanchero had a farm and family in Texas, he would not have raided his farm or taken his children captive."

"Or killed his wife?" asked the boy.

"That is true. They would have spared his family."

"But they would have killed and stolen from us Colliers, though, and captured me and Eula Bee."

He saw Grass Woman look away and then heard her soft words. "Lewallen, forget your sister, and go live in a town or fort. She'll forget you, and someday she'll be the wife of a great chief."

Lewallen said sharply, "What wife? Number one or number two or number three? Nope, I'm sticking with Mister Cabral here, and the two of us are going to keep on looking for his boy and my sister."

By now Cabral had come back to Lewallen's side. He spoke softly as Grass Woman left hurriedly. "Come on, Collier, let's get out of here! It seems I gave away my trade goods for almost nothing but the worst news a man can hear. Just about all I got to show for my work here is you."

"But Tom's alive!"

"I sure hope he is. Let's make tracks now before some other folks here decide they'd like *all* my blankets and *all* of your beads. The young braves don't know me, remember, and the Comanches ain't so inclined to let their chief tell them how to behave as other tribes are. The way I see it, Yellow Wolf is my only friend right now. And it seems to me that blue-eyed wife of Many Horses ain't no good friend to you anymore. Do you think she'll stop her husband from following us for the trade goods we gave her?"

"Yes, I do—for the beads and blanket and because of some things I said to her."

"I sure hope you're right, Collier."

TEN

Blue Coats and Bugles

Singing "Lorena" to impress the Comanches with his courage, Lewallen rode away northward from the Indian camp with Cabral, whose face was set in lines of sorrow. He said not one word until they camped that night miles from Yellow Wolf's band.

Lewallen was the one who made the fire and the evening meal of bacon and biscuits. Cabral seemed to have retreated into a silence so deep that he was afraid to speak to him.

Finally he got up the courage to say, "Mister Cabral, thank you for all you did for me back there. I'm sorry as can be about Angelita. Maybe if I would've stayed in the camp, I could've helped her. That is, if the Indians would have let me."

Cabral waited until a coyote in the distance had finished his wailing, then said heavily, "No, they wouldn't have let you, and you couldn't have helped her anyhow."

Lewallen added as he spread blankets for himself and Cabral on the ground, "It must have been real bad for Tom when she was sick. He'll sure be glad to see you when we catch up to Small Buffalo. He was expecting to see me maybe, but not you."

Cabral's big hands hung down limp over his knees as he spoke. "I don't want to talk no more about my daughter, do you hear? And I don't want to hear that song you sing again neither, because it's going to remind me of what Yellow Wolf said from now on."

"Sure, I understand." Lewallen bit back what he wanted to say about finding Eula Bee, feeling it might strike him wrong. Instead he asked, "Are we on the trail of Small Buffalo?"

"That we are. We're northward bound. That's where Kiowas range mostly, closer to New Mexico Territory."

Trying to make conversation, Lewallen asked, "Why do the Indians move around so much?"

"It's in their nature. They're wanderers. You and me, we're settlers. Wanderers and settlers sometimes get in the way of each other, and then there's trouble. Now let's get some sleep, kid. I know what's buzzing around in your head: your sister and how you can get her back. When we find the Kiowas and I buy back Tomás, I plan to ask him some more about the gambling game Yellow Wolf had with the Comanche chief from up north on the Staked Plains." Cabral shook his head. "Queer thing about that, Collier. Yellow Wolf didn't tell me the name of that chief. He should've boasted about his important visitor. I wanted to ask Yellow Wolf his name, but he got off onto a long speech about how I ought to get rid of you. He said you were bad medicine, a pony thief, and a trouble bringer. After you left the camp the sickness came."

"What?" Lewallen asked, astonished. "Did he think I caused it?"

"I reckon that he did. He was put out with you because

you stole his pony and because you didn't take to the thought of turning Comanche. Tell me, how good was my son's Comanche when you left him last year?"

"He was learning it, Mister Cabral."

"Good, maybe he'll know the name of the chief that's got your sister. How'd you like to learn some Spanish? I'll try to teach you. It'll give me something to keep my mind off Angelita. How would that suit you?"

As he sat under a pale spring moon, Lewallen's mind wandered to Mrs. Claiborne, the most gentle lady he had ever known. As a teacher, she'd tell him to jump at the chance to learn whatever he could. "You bet. It would suit me just fine, Mister Cabral. I'd like to know some Spanish. It sounds pretty when folks talk it." Trying to make more conversation, Lewallen asked, "How come you talk English so good?"

"My father was born in Mexico, but my mother was half Irish."

Lewallen said lamely, "Us Colliers thought your ma was an American lady. And we didn't know you were a New Mexican or a Comanchero. I never heard of Comancheros till I met you. I see now that I would never have made it back out of Yellow Wolf's camp by myself. So thank you again. Have you got some more family back in Sante Fe or New Mexico Territory?"

"I don't know." Cabral turned his head away from the fire so Lewallen could no longer see his face.

Afterward Lewallen fell silent out of respect for his sorrow. Apparently Cabral had led a strange sort of life. He wondered if the man missed being a Comanchero. That ought to have been a very exciting line of work, all right, though folks in Fort Belknap didn't seem to fancy it much.

They continued riding northward. Cabral said very little, but at times he pointed to marks that he said were the trail of Small Buffalo, Snow Moon, Tomás, and the two young Comanche warriors accompanying Small Buffalo. The signs Cabral saw were faint because there were so few Indians in the party. Lewallen was sure he could never have trailed them alone. These Indians were moving swiftly and not pausing to hunt along the way.

"They want to get to the main Kiowa camp fast," Cabral told Lewallen their third night away from Yellow Wolf's band.

"I reckon Small Buffalo wants to set eyes on his kinfolk again," Lewallen told Cabral sourly. "He probably wants to brag to them about the latest brave things he did, so he can get to wear a red sash. That's what Grass Woman said he wants."

"A red sash, huh? They ain't to be trifled with—them ten red-sash Kiowas."

Lewallen couldn't resist saying, "Well, I trifled with Small Buffalo once, and I'm still here to talk about it."

"It ain't a thing I'd try twice, Collier." Then Cabral added, "I think you'd better stay behind and let me go alone to see Small Buffalo in the Kiowa camp. I'll give him the message from Yellow Wolf and your poke of beads for the pony you took out of his herd after I ransom my boy back."

Lewallen paused, thinking, before he put another dry buffalo chip onto their campfire. Cabral had a point all right. While Small Buffalo visited Many Horses and Yellow

Wolf in their camp, the proud young warrior didn't dare disgrace himself by attacking an unarmed slave boy. But what was to stop the Kiowa from killing Lewallen Collier now that he was simply an enemy white man among Kiowas, his own tribe?

"Would it be easier for you if I stayed out of sight and we met later on somewhere else?"

"It would. Your being with me could make the difference between my getting Tomás back or not. Seeing you might put Small Buffalo's back up so high that he wouldn't sell me my son, no matter how much trade goods I offered him."

"Yes, it might at that." Lewallen let out a small sigh. "All right, where shall I hide out?"

"I don't know yet. I'll tell you where when I get the Kiowa camp located."

Lewallen saw how Cabral, who lay on his back with his head resting on his saddle, was staring up at the sky. Cabral said, "The moon's got a ring around her. Rain's on the way. I figure we'll find the Kiowa camp pretty soon now that we're getting closer to the border of New Mexico Territory. I know this flat country from old times here."

"Mister Cabral, can I ask you something?" Lewallen asked, as he knelt at the fire ready to bank it with dirt for the night.

"All right, ask me, if you've a mind to."

"Will you promise me to come back and get me after you ransom Tom from Small Buffalo? You won't just leave me and ride away with Tom, will you?"

Cabral remained quiet for a time, then said softly, "I could do that, but I won't. I'll come back so Tom can tell you what he knows about your baby sister and who's got her." Slowly Cabral sat up, leaning back on his elbows, looking at Lewallen. "I'll try hard as I can to do that, but if for some reason I don't, I want to fix up something for you right here and now." Grumbling at the pain the movements caused him in his wounded thigh and hip, Cabral sat up. Lewallen watched him fumble inside his shirt and pull out a long piece of leather, hold it in front of him, and untie it. There was something hanging from it, something light in color that looked like a piece of bone.

Cabral held it out to him. "Take this, Collier, and put it around your neck. It's something I had given to me by somebody a long, long time back."

Lewallen arose, came over, and took the thong from the man's hand. What he had thought was a bone was a rock, a small white one with two natural holes in it that the thong went through. It was sure a queer-looking kind of necklace.

"Is it Indian?"

"No, it ain't. It was a joke, something my brother Francisco gave me when we was boys your age. He found it. If he's still alive, he'll remember it. If I don't come back from the Kiowa camp by the time it's dark, make your way to Santa Fe and find him, Francisco Quintero."

"Not Cabral?"

"No, Quintero."

"Why should I go to him instead of to the Claibornes at the fort?"

"Because my brother Francisco perhaps could help find your sister, and Captain Claiborne never could."

"Is your brother a soldier, too?"

"No, I'm sure of that. He's an old man by now. Tell my brother about my family here in Texas. He'll find someone who will understand what you say if he has forgotten the English he learned from our mother."

"Mister Cabral, is he a Comanchero?"

"No, but he'll know men who might be. I hear that the trading still goes on."

"Thank you kindly," Lewallen told Cabral, as he put the thong over his head and let the white rock drop onto his breastbone. He couldn't imagine Cabral as a boy and having a brother who'd given him such a present. Yet it was the kind of thing Daniel might have done if he'd run across a funny-looking two-hole stone like this one in the creek bottom back home. With a pang Lewallen realized that he had no token, no memento, of Daniel at all.

He told Cabral, "I'll give it back to you so you can give it to Tom to wear after you come back from the Kiowas."

Two mornings later, after only about an hour's ride in a light rain, Cabral sent Lewallen climbing to the top of an oak in a stand of trees to look out over the countryside to the west. From the top of the tree Lewallen saw lines of smoke rising from a shallow hollow on the prairie. He guessed the smoke came from the cooking fires of Indian lodges.

When he'd reported the smoke to Cabral, he nodded somberly and said, "As long as you're off your horse, give me your poke of beads for Small Buffalo so I can pay him for the black pony. Afterward, I want you to stay in the trees out of sight and wait for me."

"Yes, Mister Cabral, if that's what you want me to do."

"It's what I want, Collier."

Lewallen opened the saddlebag nearest to him, took out a poke of beads, and handed it up to Cabral, who put the small bag into the bosom of his shirt.

"Be careful, Mister Cabral." Lewallen tried to smile but only managed a twisted grin. "Don't bother to give my kind regards to Small Buffalo." He reached up his hand to his old neighbor and said, "Please, Mister Cabral, I'd like to shake your hand before you go, and I want to wish you good luck."

"*Gracias*, Collier." Cabral's big hand was wet with rain and cold as ice.

For a time Lewallen walked the blue roan up and down among the trees. Then he sat down beneath one of them, leaning against it while his horse grazed, hobbled, nearby. He wasn't hungry enough to eat and didn't dare make a fire, and he was too nervous to take a nap. What he should have right now, when he was at such loose ends, he told himself, was one of Mrs. Claiborne's readers. He could set his mind to struggling with words.

Lewallen was asking himself what day of the week it was and what Mrs. Claiborne was making the kids study right now, when all at once he heard a familiar sound that made him smile.

A bugle call! He was really daydreaming of Fort Belknap all right to be hearing that. Mrs. Claiborne complained that the Army ran its whole day by bugle calls—and everybody else's day, too. She said there was a bugle call for just about everything a soldier did, from getting up to going to bed.

There it came again! This time, though, the bugling

brought Lewallen to his feet at the same instant his horse jerked up its head. It wasn't a daydream. It was real if the roan had heard it, too. But where was it coming from?

For certain there wasn't any fort near where he was right now. He could see the whole countryside for miles from the top of the oak.

Unhobbling the roan and grabbing his reins, Lewallen ran to the edge of the grove and cautiously looked out onto the prairie. Then he ran through the oaks to the other side. Nothing. Nothing at all. He tethered the roan and climbed up the tallest tree once more.

There! Out on the prairie, riding swiftly out of the gray mist to the southwest was a band of horsemen. Not Indians —not riding in pairs. Troopers, and they'd come out of nowhere fast, too! Straining his eyes to see through the rain, Lewallen made out a soldier at the head of a column carrying a flag.

He sucked in his breath as all at once he guessed their destination and their errand. The Kiowa camp! He heard the bugling once more. It was a call he didn't recognize, but he suspected it was a battle order. He knew Captain Claiborne's soldiers hadn't been sent out to attack the Indians, but there were other forts in Texas and New Mexico Territory. Because the soldiers were riding so hard, Lewallen was sure they were bent on attacking something. He looked out over the countryside once more, wondering if there were other enemy soldiers about and a battle might be going to happen, but there were no other riders on the prairie. Only the troopers and the camp of Kiowas.

Then he remembered. Cabral was there now! And the soldiers meant to ride down on the Indian camp.

He had to stop the soldiers! Hurrying down the oak as

fast as he could, Lewallen untied his horse, mounted, and rode out of the grove. Though he urged the roan to its top speed, by the time Lewallen was in the vicinity of the troopers they were too far ahead of him to catch up. He shouted at them with all the force of his lungs, but no one paid any attention to him. No trooper even looked back over the prairie, although Lewallen had gotten close enough to see that the coats they wore were blue not gray. Yankee troopers—enemy soldiers!

Lewallen Collier arrived at the Kiowa camp only minutes after the blue-coat troopers rode through the lodges, shooting and slashing. By the time he arrived, much of the soldiers' bloody work was done, and the rain-soaked grass of the camp was covered with the dead and wounded bodies of Kiowa braves, who had tried to defend themselves but had been taken by surprise. Women were running about, shrieking, throwing themselves onto the bodies of their men while children wailed in the entryways of the tepees. Noise-maddened ponies dashed through the camp, jumping corpses, while the dogs ran at their heels in a frenzy of yapping.

Lewallen sat the roan in a trance of horror, watching the cavalrymen darting around the lodges, firing at any man or boy they saw.

Lewallen couldn't spot Cabral or Tomás in the mass of fleeing Kiowas and firing troopers. He stood as tall as he could in his stirrups and shouted out over the din, "Hey, Mister Cabral, it's me! Lewallen Collier!"

A soldier on a bay horse came riding past him, gazed at him, shocked, and reined in, making his horse rear and paw the air. When it came down, he said, "You ain't a

Kiowa! Who in the devil are you, and where did you come from?"

"Lewallen Collier from Palo Duro County. I came here riding after you because my pardner, Mister Cabral, is here somewhere in the camp."

"Well, get yourself out of the line of fire or somebody'll shoot you." The trooper reached out and with a quirt taken from his boot lashed Lewallen's horse on the right hip, sending it bounding forward and away across the path of a young screaming Kiowa woman, knocking her to the ground.

His heart pounding in fright and sick to his stomach, Lewallen watched the fight from the edge of the camp, obeying the trooper's order. He couldn't think of anything but what was going on in front of him. He tried to pray, but the words wouldn't come. The only thing he could think of at all was the raid on his own farm. As a trooper grabbed up a burning stick from a fire and threw it into the entryway of a tepee, the image of his own burning cabin rose up in Lewallen's memory, and he groaned.

At last the crackling sound of shooting was over and was replaced by wailings of the Indian women and children, who would later be taken prisoner by the troopers.

Lewallen stayed where he was and waited until a soldier came riding over to him. "Major Redigote wants to talk with you now, boy," he said.

"Yes, sir." Minding his manners with great care among these enemy Yankees, Lewallen walked his roan back to the camp, following the trooper. The soldier led him to a handsome sorrel. There were gold colored straps on the rider's shoulders that showed he was an officer.

"I'm Major Redigote, United States Army, son," he snapped at Lewallen. "Who are you? Why are you here?"

"Lewallen Collier of Palo Duro County, sir. I came up here to these parts with a friend and pardner by the name of Cabral. He rode in here today to buy his son back from a Kiowa who had him as a slave."

"Cabral, huh? A Mexican? Are you Mexican?"

"No. Mister Cabral used to be my neighbor. Indians took his two kids and me and my little sister captives last year. His girl died this past winter in the Comanche camp. Mister Cabral was helping me to get my sister back just now. He was going to ask his boy about her once he'd got him ransomed from the Kiowa."

"Why didn't you ask the Army to do that for you?"

"I did, sir. I went to Fort Belknap and asked them there."

"Confederates, eh? And they couldn't help you? Well, that doesn't surprise me. Our Indian scouts told me that they believed there was a captive in this camp, maybe more. They saw a white child here five days ago. We came riding after this band because they killed three entire families some fifty miles away."

Lewallen's heart gave a sickening leap. A white child? Eula Bee? Could she have been here among the Kiowas with Small Buffalo and Tomás? "Was it a girl the scout saw and was she a redhead, sir?"

"I don't know. I don't recall their saying what color hair the child had."

Lewallen said, "I reckon the Kiowas here might have had white slaves the way the Comanches did. How about Mister Cabral? Where's he now?"

"I don't know. I didn't see anyone here but Kiowas.

Trooper Gray," Redigote spoke to a passing rider, "escort this lad through the camp—he's looking for some people he knows—and keep your eyes open for any white children here. Look in the lodges. They could be hidden in there."

"Yes, sir. Come with me, boy." A long horse pistol cocked and ready in his hand, the young soldier led the way on horseback away from the major, and Lewallen followed him.

"Mister Cabral! Mister Cabral!" Lewallen cried out, as the two of them rode among the lodges.

There was never a reply to his call, though he made it again and again.

At last Lewallen found Cabral and Tomás in the center of the Kiowa camp. Both were dead. Cabral was shot through the head and Tomás through the chest. Tomás was clasped in his father's embrace, so Lewallen knew that the two had been reunited before the soldiers struck. He guessed at what happened. The Yankees had attacked. Tomás had been shot first. Seeing him, Cabral had run to him and grabbed him to his chest. Then he had been shot down, too.

"That's them—them two," Lewallen told the young trooper through a blur of tears. He looked to the side of Cabral and saw a gray-haired Kiowa lying, sprawled on his face, a lance in his hand, just outside the entryhole of a tepee. A red sash was wound about his waist. Near the Kiowa lay a woman who probably was one of his wives. She was staring up at the rain-spitting sky. In his heart, Lewallen guessed them to be Small Buffalo's father and mother. Grass Woman had said his father was a red-sash warrior. The presence of Tom Cabral's body must mean that this lodge was theirs.

What about Small Buffalo? Was he here, too? Had he been shot, too? Where was Snow Moon?

A deep groaning came from the tepee. Lewallen dismounted. Trooper Gray got off his horse an instant later, pushed Lewallen out of the way with his pistol barrel, went inside first, then shouted out, "Come on in, kid. There's more Indians in here!"

Lewallen bent low and went into the tepee. There were two Indians inside, a Kiowa and a Comanche. But the Kiowa wasn't Small Buffalo. He was a white-haired old man lying crumpled on a pile of pelts. The Comanche lay with his blood-smeared hands over his abdomen. Lewallen knew him as a young brave of Yellow Wolf's band, someone who had been a member of the war party that had taken Eula Bee and him captive.

The badly wounded Comanche stared up at Lewallen in amazed silence as Lewallen spoke to the trooper. "I came here looking for my baby sister, besides Mister Cabral and his boy. Can you talk in sign language and ask this Comanche where my sister is and what Comanche band she's with?"

"Sure, I'll try some sign language on him, but I don't think he's in the mood to answer."

Lewallen looked on in the dimness of the lodge as the trooper knelt on one knee and made gestures to the Indian, who never moved his hands from his abdomen. The Comanche kept his gaze fixed on the soldier's face. Finally, though, his eyes rolled toward Lewallen again.

The Indian opened his mouth and with effort gasped out only two words, "*Ekapi. Tasiwoo.*"

Lewallen's mind raced as the meaning of the words stunned him. For a moment he thought he might fall down beside the wounded Indian.

Ekapi he knew meant "redhead." *Tasiwoo* meant "buffalo." There was only one possible connection to be made from the two words. The Kiowa had Eula Bee! Lewallen said, "He's saying that a Kiowa by the name of Small Buffalo has my sister now."

Of course, Small Buffalo had Eula Bee Collier!

Yellow Wolf had been protecting his Kiowa son-in-law from Lewallen by not telling Cabral that Small Buffalo had Eula Bee. He had made up the gambling story to throw Lewallen off her track. The peace chief had tried to get Cabral to stop traveling with Lewallen, saying Lewallen was "bad medicine." Yellow Wolf knew that if Lewallen was with Cabral when the Comanchero found Small Buffalo, he would offer ransom for Eula Bee. Yellow Wolf expected Cabral to ransom Tom, but after all he was only a slave boy. Eula Bee was, on the other hand, considered a daughter now, a daughter to Snow Moon, who'd lost her second infant last winter.

Lewallen knew the Kiowa had always fancied Eula Bee and wanted her. The vision of Eula Bee playing with his necklace as he held her in front of him after he'd killed Ma and Daniel and Uncle Joshua rose in Lewallen's memory, sickening him.

His sister and Small Buffalo!

"Ask him where Small Buffalo is?" Lewallen begged the young Yankee trooper.

The soldier made more sign-language gestures, and the Comanche watched him, but this time he didn't speak. Instead he lifted one red-stained hand. As his blood came gushing out of his abdomen, he made a gesture that resembled a snake gliding backward.

The Yankee got to his feet and stared at Lewallen in a puzzled manner. "I think that was sign language for his own tribe, the Comanches. They're called the Snakes Moving Backward by the other Indians. It appears that he's saying that this Small Buffalo is with the Comanches, not with the Kiowas."

"Maybe he is. He moves around a good bit," said Lewallen.

"Well, boy, this Comanche won't be telling us anything more. He just died. I don't think he was lying to you. He realized he was dying. I take it you know this Small Buffalo by sight?"

"Yes, I know him."

"Well, what do you say we get out and look around the camp for him? On second thought, the Comanche might only have been telling me that he was a Comanche. Well, that's something we won't ever know for sure. If you don't find Small Buffalo in this camp, we could question the Kiowa women about him."

Looking down at the two dead Indians, Lewallen spoke aloud what he felt to be true, "Small Buffalo isn't here, but he was. He gave his boy slave, the dead boy outside the tepee, to the care of his father, the man with the red sash. I think Small Buffalo's moved on already, traveling to another Comanche band he knows. It won't do any good to ask the other Kiowas here about him. They won't tell us.

They think mighty highly of him. He's gone away with his wife, and he's got my sister with him."

Trooper Gray shook his head, then pushed out of the lodge into the rain.

Lewallen asked him outside, "Will the troopers be burying Mister Cabral and his boy, Tom?"

"I suspect so. The major will probably detail some men to do that chore."

"I owe that to Mister Cabral," Lewallen said with a nod. "He helped to bury my ma and my little brother and great uncle back home after the Comanches killed them last year. Mister Cabral came here to trade. He had his horse and two pack mules with him. He's got a brother in Santa Fe he talked to me about. If your major would let me have Cabral's three animals to take back to Santa Fe to him, I'd be much obliged."

"Maybe he will. You could go to Santa Fe now. The Union Army just took it back from the Confederates this very month, and we're driving the Rebels out of the territory now. What side was Cabral on? Did he side with the Union or the Confederates?"

"I don't know." Lewallen paused beside his horse, staring at the soldier. "I can't recall ever asking him what side he favored. All he wanted was to be left alone down on his farm. He used to be a Comanchero a long time back."

"One of them Indian traders? Well then, good riddance to him. You ought to be glad you aren't hooked up with him any longer. If he was a Comanchero, he was as bad in my book as any Indian on these plains."

Under his breath Lewallen whispered, "I knew him—and you didn't."

ELEVEN

Behind the Closed Gate

Trooper Gray escorted Lewallen back to the major, and Lewallen told him of his search for Eula Bee and his belief that she had been here in the Kiowa camp. When he finished, the officer called one of his Indian scouts to him and questioned him in English. The scout was a Tonkawa, a tribe that was an enemy of the Comanches. The Tonkawa, who spoke understandable English, told them that the child he'd seen here was a girl and a redhead. Her hair had blazed like fire. He'd spotted her walking about with a young slender Indian woman. Snow Moon? Snow Moon and Eula Bee.

When Lewallen asked to search the camp for Small Buffalo, the major sent him off with Trooper Gray and a sergeant.

As Lewallen bent over to examine the dead Kiowa males and looked among the frightened, weeping women who were being assembled along with the girl children, he grew sicker and sicker at the sight of the slaughter. Small Buffalo was not there among the dead. He didn't know any of these Kiowas, but their closed, cold faces wrenched at his heart.

On his return to the major, Lewallen reported, "Small Buffalo is not here, sir." He'd thought hard as he walked back to the officer and added, "I guess I've lost Eula Bee for good this time. I saw my pardner's pack mules and horse just now. If it's all right with you, I'd like to take them to his kinfolk in Santa Fe." He paused, hoping the Yankee would agree. He was careful not to mention tracking Small Buffalo, for he doubted if the major would permit him to ride off by himself to look for him.

Major Redigote nodded, then said, "You're right about your sister. You'd best try to forget her. You can't go off after her by yourself. God only knows where she is by now. These captive Kiowa women won't tell us where she went even if they knew. Where are your own folks?"

"They're all gone except for Eula Bee and me. The Indians killed everyone but us two kids." No, he wouldn't tell the Yankee officer that his pa and Johnny were fighting for the Confederacy. "Mister Cabral told me if he didn't come back from trying to ransom his boy that I ought to go to Santa Fe and tell his kin what happened. Sir, Mister Cabral would want me to take his goods to his family rather than have somebody who has no right to his animals get hold of them."

"All right. It's irregular to let you do that, but this kind of fighting is irregular, too." The major looked about him at the smoldering lodges with distaste. "Kill all the males. Take the women prisoners. That's the kind of orders I'll be getting these days now that the Confederates have been driven out of New Mexico Territory. We Union Army men are guarding the frontier now. I hate the kind of fighting we did here. It's degrading to a soldier. Women and girls—captives. Fah!" The major shot a stream of tobacco juice down onto the grass, then added, "All right, son. You can ride with us as far as Fort Union, our headquarters, and make your own way from there to Santa Fe. It isn't far from our fort."

"Thank you kindly, sir." Lewallen was about to turn away when the officer called out to him.

"What kind of folks are your partner's family?"

"Traders," Lewallen said. Then he added, "Storekeepers." He wouldn't say Comancheros because of what Captain Claiborne had hinted back at Fort Belknap and because of what Trooper Gray had just said. He asked, "Sir, could I say a couple of words over Mister Cabral and Tom before we go? I saw a while back that some of your men were digging a hole near where they were killed."

"Yes, but don't take long about it."

"I won't. Are you going to bury the Kiowas, too?"

"No, no more than they bury the bodies of the settlers they murder."

"Yes, sir." Lewallen went and stood beside the lodge where the Cabrals had met their deaths.

He looked on as the grave was dug and the troopers came up out of it. Then he took two of the bright blankets from inside the lodge that he'd recognized as Cabral's trade blankets and dropped one of them into the grave.

He told the soldiers, "They were neighbors and friends of mine. The blankets belonged to the man. I'd thank you kindly if you'd put them down there together on the one blanket. I'll throw this other one over them. Afterward you can fill in the hole."

"Sure, kid, but they won't be needing the blankets to keep them warm down there."

Lewallen was silent while the man he'd once hated and his son were dropped into the grave. Then, still kneeling, he put the second blanket over the Cabrals, arose, and stood back as the grave was filled in with dirt.

He waited until the soldiers had left, then he took off his hat, holding it over his chest, and said, "I'm sorry about how things turned out. *Gracias* for everything you both did for me. I hope you get to Heaven in good shape." Then he mumbled the Lord's Prayer as well as he could remember it from his ma's teaching. He'd never been able to get all the words to heart just exactly right, but he did the best he could.

Just as he finished, Trooper Gray came by and Lewallen asked, "Would you please not tell anybody else that Mister Cabral used to be a Comanchero?"

"Why not, kid?"

"So they won't cuss him now that he's dead and gone."

"All right, it's between the two of us then. If it makes you feel any better, I won't tell anybody what he was."

After roping Cabral's black horse and two pack mules in a long line, one behind the other, Lewallen mounted the blue roan. He saw the troopers ride in from shooting the Kiowa ponies in their pasture and sat watching the soldiers on foot gathering Kiowa women and children into a long double line of captives.

The rain had turned into a downpour by now, soaking Indian prisoners and troopers alike to the skin.

Lewallen waited while Major Redigote took his position in the lead beside the bugler, standard bearer, and Tonkawa scouts and the other soldiers mounted up and swung into line behind them. The double file of captives was escorted on each side by a line of troopers on horseback. Behind them came even more blue-coated cavalrymen.

When everyone had started out, Lewallen clucked to his horse and rode forward to take his place behind the soldiers. Leading Cabral's horse and mules, he was last of all to take the trail to Santa Fe.

He didn't look behind him at the sickening ruin that was the Kiowa camp of unburied dead and fired tepees. Eula Bee had been here, and he'd lost her. Tom Cabral and his father had been here, and he'd lost them, too. He felt he had almost as much reason to weep as the Kiowa women.

As he saw it, he had only one hope—the Comancheros of New Mexico Territory. At least, that was what Cabral had thought.

With one wet, chilly hand Lewallen groped inside his shirt and got hold of Cabral's little white rock. Still holding it, he turned in his saddle and looked behind him, not at the burning lodges, but at Cabral's big black horse and pack mules.

Lewallen didn't spend much time at Fort Union. This fort, unlike Fort Belknap, was mostly built of wood that was too green, so the buildings had warped out of shape. As a matter of fact, Fort Union was still being built. While he was there, soldiers were at work, making a star-shaped fortification of wood and adobe. Their pounding and hammering made the fort a mighty noisy place. When a person's ears weren't aching from bugle calls and the shouts of marching orders from the parade ground, they ached from all the clatter of building.

After a day's rest Lewallen asked Major Redigote to write a letter to Mr. Francisco Quintero saying that "Lewallen Collier was entitled to convey the pack mules and horse of his now-dead partner, Joseph Cabral, to the man's relatives in Santa Fe."

After he wrote the letter, Redigote's words to Lewallen were, "My advice to you is to give the animals and goods to this man in Sante Fe and then settle down there yourself. I doubt that there'll be any more fighting in New Mexico Territory between us and the Rebels. We won a battle there last month, and we've chased the Rebels out of Santa Fe. If the War lasts until you're old enough, you can enlist out here just as easily as back East."

Lewallen knew it wouldn't be a smart thing to say that he was a Rebel and if he ever joined any army it would be the Confederate one. He asked, though, "Is there any way I could let the folks at Fort Belknap know what happened to Mister Cabral and that I'm all right?"

"I don't see how I could do that for you. I don't feel one bit friendly toward the Rebels at this moment. After all they won two battles back East last summer, Bull Run and Ball's Bluff, and we haven't won anything there yet. No, I cannot write letters to Confederates—not even about you."

"No, I guess not." Lewallen thought of the Claibornes. He was sure they had written to his pa about all the things he'd told them about. They'd probably also written his pa by now that he'd gone off with Cabral to ransom his kids and Eula Bee. Well, there wasn't anything he could do about what the Claibornes chose to write, though none of the news would exactly comfort Pa when he had their letters read out loud to him. Pa had never learned to read himself.

The major's next words to Lewallen were, "Go to school in Santa Fe, and if that isn't possible, try to find some suitable work."

"Yes, sir," Lewallen told him. "Thank you. I think I might try to find some work, trading most likely. Trading and farming are about all I know how to do."

"They can be good work, both of them. One last word of advice to you. Don't ever take up soldiering as your life's work. I don't like to make war on women and children. Meet the Indian braves on the open prairie in a true battle, yes, indeed, but shooting up a camp full of women and young ones, no!"

"No, sir, I don't plan to be a soldier."

Lewallen's thoughts went back to the Kiowa camp as he had last seen it. He doubted if he'd ever forget the sorrowing women carrying their children on that rain-swept trail from their village. They'd wailed anew as they'd been herded into guarded stockades when they arrived at the fort. These Kiowa women and kids were prisoners of the Yankees. And nobody was going to set them to guarding ponies so they could escape to another band of Kiowas or Comanche allies somewhere on the prairies. He had no idea what would become of these Kiowa captives.

Lewallen left Fort Union in the company of two New

Mexican traders who had brought food supplies to the troopers and who were now on their way home to Santa Fe. The younger one spoke fairly good English. He dropped back to ride beside Lewallen some miles from the fort and asked, "How much silver do you want for the black one?" And he jerked his head toward Cabral's big horse.

"He's not for sale. Besides, he doesn't belong to me," Lewallen returned rudely. He wanted to travel with these well-armed men but not to talk with them on the way. He didn't aim to get into any more palavers with anybody about Comancheros.

The young man shrugged his shoulders, then spurred his horse on ahead to join his fellow trader. Lewallen heard him talking Spanish to the other man and heard the older trader snort, then laugh. Sure as shooting they were talking about him and his bad manners, but they finally stopped speaking and rode along together in silence, ignoring him.

Lewallen would have welcomed quiet from any traveling companions now. Even if Daniel or Johnny had been with him, he would have hushed them up if he could. It was because the land he was passing through awed him. What he saw struck him dumb with wonder.

Mountains, what astonishing, overwhelming, remarkable things they were to him, a boy who'd never seen a mountain before. Those he spied from the Santa Fe Trail were tall ones, capped with snow on their peaks. Their enormous size made him feel very small. He marveled at the trees on their slopes, because he had never seen such trees before either. Some of them were evergreens; others were covered with leaves that trembled in the slightest of breezes, looking like bits of silver. There was no flat prairie here, nothing but rolling green countryside dotted with thousands of small, dark-green bushes. Among the bushes wild flowers were blooming. How beautiful it was, beautiful and strange and sweetly scented.

Still enchanted by the countryside, Lewallen was greatly surprised when he recognized the sound of bells. He heard the old city of Santa Fe before he saw it. The music of bells rang out clearly in the sharp air, but he didn't know where the sound was coming from. For a moment he thought of calling ahead to ask the young man who spoke English, but he thought better of it. That might lead to more conversation.

Did the bells belong to churches somewhere in the far distance? Or to schools? If they were church and school bells in Santa Fe, it must be a very large place to have so many.

Even so, as they entered in dim twilight, the city astounded Lewallen by its great size, by the strange shapes of its many big adobe buildings and its large number of churches, from whose belltowers the bells were constantly ringing. Santa Fe wasn't one bit like Palo Duro, a town of one street. Here many streets led off from the plaza where the enormous rambling Palace of the Governors stood and where the most important shops and other businesses were located.

Lewallen sat his horse in the center of the plaza, making other riders go around him and Cabral's animals as darkness came down. All the time he was wondering how he would find Francisco Quintero among so many folks. If only he knew more Spanish. He was afraid to make a fool of himself by trying out those few words Cabral had taught him.

Lewallen waited, watching people go by him, until a tiny old woman with a black shawl pulled up over her head and shoulders started past him. Then he asked, *"Por favor, la casa de Francisco Quintero?"*

She didn't open the shawl so he could see her face, but she stopped and nodded. Then she called out to a boy walking toward her, spoke to him in Spanish, pointed to Lewallen, and hurried on her way past the governor's palace. The black-haired boy, who wore a leather jacket and leather knee-length breeches, came up to Lewallen's roan and looked questioningly at Lewallen. "Francisco Quintero?" he asked. When Lewallen nodded, the boy took hold of the bridle of Lewallen's horse and led it out of the plaza down a narrow side street.

How that street turned and twisted before it led into another one and then another. At last the boy stopped and pointed directly ahead of him.

"Gracias," said Lewallen to the boy, who moved away into the shadows of an intersecting street.

Lewallen found himself in front of a high adobe wall with a wooden gate set into it. He dismounted, hit the gate with his fist, and waited.

Someone came soon. Judging from the glow over the wall, the figure came by lantern light. A man's voice called out something in Spanish.

Lewallen shouted back, "Francisco Quintero. I want to see Francisco Quintero."

A tiny panel in the gate slid back, and Lewallen knew

he was being examined by watchful eyes. "*Que?*" came the voice.

Lewallen repeated, "Francisco Quintero. Joseph Quintero sent me to his brother, Francisco. Here, wait a minute, *por favor.*" With one hand he got hold of the white rock, pulled its thong off over his head, and handed it through the panel. "For Francisco Quintero," he told the man on the other side. "This is from his brother, Joseph Quintero."

"*Ah, si,*" the panel slid shut, and Lewallen could hear slow footsteps going away.

He waited and waited, leaning up against the adobe wall, in the darkness. What would he do if nobody came back to the gate at all? He supposed the best thing then for him to do would be to go back to the Palace of the Governors and return the black horse and pack mules to someone there to give to Francisco Quintero. Afterward he'd sell his beads and needles here, hole up somehow, and try to ponder some other way to reach Eula Bee.

Suddenly his ears caught tapping sounds coming toward the gate. Then the panel opened again, and a deeper voice asked in English, "Who are you? Where did you find this white stone?"

"Lewallen Collier of Palo Duro County in Texas. I was pardner to Mister Joe Cabral of the same county. He used to be a Comanchero, he told me. He told me, too, that he had a brother here in Santa Fe by the name of Francisco Quintero."

"Where is Joseph Cabral?"

"Dead. We were trading together with some Kiowa Indians. I brought his pack mules and horse with me to give back to his brother Francisco if I can find him."

"Did the Kiowas kill Joseph Cabral then?"

"No, the Yankee troopers killed him and his boy, Tom, when they attacked the Indian camp. The Yankees didn't mean to shoot him. They didn't know he was in the camp trading. I tried to stop the soldiers, but I couldn't."

"Yes." There was a very long silence, then a command in Spanish, and the gate swung slowly open.

A tall old man dressed in dark cloth and a white shirt stood leaning on two canes between two lantern-bearing Indian men in long white tunics. The old man said, "Welcome to Casa Quintero. Come in and bring the horse and mules with you. My servants will put them in the stables with your animal. Please to come with me now.'

Lewallen went inside and surrendered the reins of the four animals to the servants, as another man closed and barred the gate, then went on ahead with a lantern across the courtyard.

Lewallen came behind the old man, who walked with great difficulty. Was he Cabral's brother? he wondered.

He asked, "Are you Francisco Quintero?"

"Yes, I am Francisco Quintero. Come into my house, eat, and tell me of my youngest brother and why he gave you his stone."

"Yes, sir, I will, but it's a long story."

"They are often the best kind. I have the time."

The house Lewallen entered was the finest he had ever seen, but its white-washed, thick walls and heavy, black furniture seemed strange to him. At the request of the old man he sat down in a leather-bottomed chair across the table from him.

"Bring food and drink for this boy," the old man ordered a woman servant in a yellow blouse and long, blue, flounced skirt. While Lewallen drank two cups of thick chocolate and ate a plate of highly spiced meat, he thought about how he ought to talk to this old man who didn't seem to be even spry enough to ride a horse, let alone be a trader.

He finished eating and started to talk. "Us Colliers knew your brother and his wife and two kids first under the name of Cabral, so that's what I'll call him, if you don't mind."

"Call my brother what you wish. Do you know why he left Santa Fe so many years ago? Did he tell you that?"

"Yes, sir." Lewallen saw over the candle flames that Francisco Quintero's eyes were the same green color as his brother's. He went on, "He said he killed a saloon-keeper here in Santa Fe and couldn't ever come back because of that."

"That is true. He killed the husband of our second sister, Angelita. Because of that he was no longer welcome for many years among the Quintero family. Joseph was wild as a young man."

Startled, Lewallen still went on, "All the same, he sure doted on his kids and wife. His girl was named Angelita. Well, sir, when a Comanche raiding party killed his wife and captured his kids and shot him full of arrows, he took out to trail his kids and get them back."

"What of you? How did you come to be with him?"

"I was a captive of the same Indians—me and my little sister, Eula Bee. I got away from the Comanches when I was guarding ponies one day, and I rode to a fort where I ran into Mister Cabral. He came there to get help from the soldiers, too. But we couldn't get their help, either one of us."

"Ah. Tell me the rest of your story."

Lewallen sat back, frowning, pouring out the tale of the months since the attack on his farm up to the deaths of Cabral and Tomás. He ended with, "Before your brother Joe rode off to the Kiowa camp to ransom Tom, he gave me the white rock and said if he didn't come back I was to ride to Santa Fe and look you up. So I did just that. There's quite a bit of trade goods still on his mules."

"*Si.*" The old man smiled slightly. "Thank you for delivering his animals to me. I am sorry that he came to such a death. What do you ask of me? How can I repay you?"

"Mister, are you a Comanchero?"

"No, I am too old and crippled for that work."

"But I need to find some Comancheros!"

"Why is that?"

"So I can go with them to buy back my sister. That's what Pa and Ma would want me to do. I know it. Mister Cabral told me that the Comancheros could help me do that."

"Ah, I thought that this is what you would want. It is your true reason for coming here to Santa Fe?"

"No, sir, not the only reason. I brought the mules and horse here, didn't I? I didn't have to tell the Yankee officer who they belonged to. I could've said they belonged to me, not to your brother. Can you put me in touch with some Comancheros here, so I can talk to them about Eula Bee?"

"Perhaps I can do that, but I will make no promise to you at this moment. Let me think about it, and in the morning I will let you know. As for tonight, you will be my guest."

Lewallen Collier heaved a sigh, then said, "All right, Mister Quintero, but please bear in mind that Eula Bee's waiting and watching for me and has been for months. I know she has."

TWELVE

The Comancheros

Lewallen was awakened the next morning from a restless sleep in a little white-walled bedchamber by the tapping of old Quintero's canes. Then the man, followed by the maidservant with a tray, parted the heavy, striped, woolen draperies over the door and entered. "You sleep late, but then you rode far yesterday. The men I wish you to see have arrived from the village of Santa Inez."

"What men?" Lewallen asked, as he sat up in the sheepskin-covered bed.

"My sons," the old man replied, as the woman put down the tray and went out. "I have reported to my sons what you told me last night about their uncle Joseph."

"Mister Quintero, can they help me?"

"Perhaps. It will be by their choice. Eat now, then come to the courtyard of the fountain." The old man went out, leaving Lewallen to dress himself, drink the hot chocolate, and eat the sweet cakes.

By daylight Lewallen found the peaceful Quintero house greatly different from any he'd ever seen. Wood had been used only for the ceiling beams and furniture. The white-washed walls were of sun-dried mud, adobe, and the floors of hard-packed earth. The roof was red tile, and long strings of braided scarlet peppers hung on walls.

After some wandering, he finally reached a courtyard where a small fountain played in the center of a pool, its waters bright in the sunlight.

Francisco Quintero and his sons sat around a table waiting for him. There was someone else present—a thin, short, black-haired boy near his own age. Like the men, he was garbed in a leather jacket, wide-brimmed, black hat, and buckskin trousers.

Quintero beckoned to Lewallen. "Come, sit down. You did not expect another boy, eh? This is my grandson, Martin."

"Pleased to meet you." Lewallen bobbed his head in greeting and sat down beside Martin on the rim of the pool.

"These are my sons." The old man recited a list of names that Lewallen couldn't entirely catch except that the oldest of the sun-bronzed four was called Pablo.

Lewallen looked from brother to brother. They were all gazing hard at him with sharp, dark eyes. He asked earnestly, "Please, I want to find my sister and get her back from the Indians. She was a captive of the Comanches, but I think she's with the Kiowas now. Can you help me?"

Pablo Quintero had a husky voice that was nearly a whisper as he spoke to his father. Lewallen could tell he was asking a question, but couldn't understand what he said.

Francisco Quintero explained. "My sons do not speak

English well. They did not have the advantage of knowing their grandmother from Ireland who spoke your language. Speak to me, and I will speak to them in Spanish."

"All right. Would you please ask them if they can help me?"

"If they wish to help they can. You see they are Comancheros."

The boy Martin touched Lewallen on the shoulder, then gave a swift, white-toothed smile and jabbed at his own chest, saying, "Si, Comancheros!"

Comancheros. The Quintero family were still Indian traders! Lewallen's heart gave a leap of hope.

"Will they help me?" he repeated.

Old Quintero spoke to his sons, then turned to Lewallen. "Pablo says they will try to buy your sister back from the Indians when he and his brothers go in July to their rendezvous with the Comanches and the Kiowas in Texas."

"In July? Why so long from now?"

"It is not long. It is April now. Pablo says he will do this because you were a partner to his uncle. He will take your trade beads with him in July and try to bring your sister back here to you in New Mexico Territory."

"He won't have to do that, Mister Quintero. When I get Eula Bee back, I'll take her to Fort Belknap. We're Texas folks, her and me."

Once more the old man spoke to his sons. Then he translated for Lewallen. "Pablo refuses to take you to the valley with them. He says it would be very foolish to take such a boy as you."

Lewallen burst out angrily, pointing to the other boy, "Does he go with them?"

"Yes, it will be Martin's first time. They will take him because he is so swift a rider."

"I can ride fast, too. I bet I can ride as fast as he can."

Francisco Quintero held up a knotted finger. "Remember. My brother refused to let you go with him into the Kiowa camp. That was wisdom on his part. Pablo thinks as wisely as Joseph did. If this Kiowa sees you among the Comancheros, do you think he would give up your sister to my sons? No. However, if you remain here, in Santa Inez where my sons live, they may be able to ransom the child. They have ransomed other American and Mexican captives from the Indians before."

Lewallen crossed his arms and thought while he listened to the fountain murmuring softly behind him. Finally he said, "All right, Mister Quintero. Tell your sons that I'll do whatever they say."

Quintero translated his decision, and all four of his sons nodded in agreement. Then as they arose to go into the house with their father, Lewallen asked the old man, "Winter's over now. How come they have to wait for July before they leave?"

"To give the Indians time to gather the cattle to trade for the goods my sons will bring."

Lewallen drew in his breath. *Cattle!* Indians didn't breed and raise cattle. Sure as the devil, the Quinteros were trading with the Indians for stolen Texas steers. They were waiting to give the Indians time to do their spring raiding. No wonder nobody in Texas liked the

Comancheros. He asked next, "What do the Indians trade the steers for, Mister Quintero?"

"Iron arrowheads, gunpowder, pistols, and whiskey."

Lewallen could scarcely contain a gasp. They were trading things to the Comanches that they could use to go out and steal more cattle—and to kill people, too.

He asked, being careful not to let his feelings show too much, "Do your sons go out every July? I was with the Comanches last summer, and the band I was with didn't go out trading."

"My sons go each July, but the same bands of Indians do not always come to the Texas valley every summer. Some years they do. Other years they stay away. But there are always Comanches and Kiowas."

"Will Small Buffalo come?"

"We do not know, but if he was not there last year, the chances are good he will come this year."

"Do your sons know him by sight?"

"Pablo says he believes he knows him, but he saw him last as a youth. He knew his father."

"And the Comanches, Yellow Wolf and Many Horses?"

"He knows them, too. By now he is acquainted with many men of the Comanches and the Kiowas. If anyone can bring your sister back to you, it will be my Pablo."

"Thanks for talking to them for me, Mister Quintero."

Lewallen eyed the Quintero boy with envy. Martin was to go out with the traders while he was to stay behind. Anger rose in Lewallen's breast.

No, sir. If Martin Quintero was going, he'd be danged if he'd cool his heels in Santa Inez while the Comancheros were out on the plains dickering for Eula Bee. That wasn't

something Pa would approve of—his ducking his duty.
Pa would expect him to think of a better way.

Santa Inez was a small, distant mountain village
populated by a few New Mexican Indians but mostly by
the Quinteros. Lewallen lived in the big crowded adobe
of Pablo Quintero. The man and his wife were kind to him
because of his partnership with Cabral. Francisco Quintero had given Cabral's big black horse to his oldest son,
who rode it often about the village.

Lewallen soon made a friend of Martin, the oldest of
the eight Quintero children and clearly their leader.
Martin took him fishing and hunting and taught Lewallen
Spanish. He taught Lewallen the Spanish word for whatever Lewallen pointed to in exchange for the English
word because, as he said, traders need to know tongues
other than their own.

By the first of June the boys were speaking to one another in a mixture of English and Spanish that baffled
everybody else in Santa Inez. They communicated with
each other so well that Lewallen was able to talk to Martin
about such matters as how he felt about losing Eula Bee.

Though Martin hadn't lost a single one of his five little
sisters, he seemed to understand very well how Lewallen
felt. He said, "It is sad that the Comanches do not have
many children of their own, but they should not take the
children of other people all the same." He nodded and
went on, "I wouldn't give up one of my sisters, not even
Lupita who pesters us."

"Martin, I *have* to get my sister back!" Lewallen told
his friend.

"You will. She will be found someday. I hope my father will find her in the valley next month."

"Our pa and ma would want me to get Eula Bee back somehow—no matter how hard it is to do it."

"I think my father and mother would want me to do the same, even for Lupita. It would be a duty. I understand. I promise you that I will try to help you if I can."

"*Gracias*, Martin. Maybe someday you can."

Throughout June, Lewallen watched the preparations the Quintero brothers made for their forthcoming journey out onto the plains. They owned a shed where they stored barrels and boxes of trade goods and kegs of New Mexico whiskey nicknamed "Taos lightning." In a nearby corral were strong young mules, and another shed sheltered a cart with two wheels, an open wagon, and a wagon with a canvas top. It was this canvas-top wagon that took Lewallen's gaze each time he passed it. Its bottom was deep in order to transport goods that were lightweight but might be damaged by rain, such as blankets, bolts of calico, sacks of sugar, tobacco, dried corn, and beans.

Lewallen had a plan in mind by now. It would be risky, but then this whole Comanchero business was.

What remained of Cabral's trade goods, as well as Lewallen's store of beads and needles, were packed into the covered wagon the evening before the Comancheros were to leave Santa Inez for Texas. Lewallen had volunteered to help them pack that particular wagon, and his offer was accepted.

The next morning Lewallen ate breakfast with the Pablo Quintero family and said adios to Pablo and to

Martin. Then, when he knew that the entire family was inside the village church praying for a safe journey, he slipped unseen out the back of their adobe and went to the covered wagon, where the mules stood waiting in their traces. He climbed up inside and burrowed under trade blankets, hiding himself and his little sack of provisions and water flask.

He prayed that the traders would be so many miles away from Santa Inez by the time he was discovered that they wouldn't send him back on foot.

He knew by now from talking with Martin much about what it meant to be a Comanchero. Comanche trading wasn't exactly a well-thought-of line of work even in New Mexico Territory, and it was downright dangerous in Texas. Because of the many soldiers in Santa Fe, Quintero's sons lived in far-off Santa Inez, where no one came prying about. If old Francisco Quintero had still been a Comanchero, he wouldn't dare live in Santa Fe, where there was a fort with soldiers nearby. The old man liked the company of educated men and often entertained priests and officials from the palace.

Martin had told Lewallen that the Comancheros never took the easy route into Texas, the well-known Santa Fe Trail, when they went off trading. Too many curious travelers and far too many soldiers used that route. The uniforms the soldiers wore would make little difference to the Quintero brothers. Soldiers in gray, Lewallen's Confederates, would have been just as quick to put Comancheros in jail as the Yankees.

Although he was secreted under a heap of trade blankets, Lewallen knew when Pablo Quintero started his caravan out of Santa Inez. He heard the cracking sound of the man's long whip and his bellowed shouts to his brothers, when they descended the steep mountain trails, to keep at a proper distance so the wagons wouldn't smash into each other.

Then came the sudden jerking as the mules surged forward in their harnesses, pulling the covered wagon, making the wheels under Lewallen's body start turning on the long journey to the trading rendezvous.

Lewallen closed his eyes and sighed. At last they were on their way to Texas! But he had to stay out of sight, never cough, never sneeze, and try not even to move his body, lest he make a noise that would alert Pablo Quintero.

Lewallen Collier waited, hidden that long first day in the covered wagon, listening eagerly for the oldest Quintero brother to shout a halt.

At last the call came. He waited until the men and Martin were seated around their campfire, cooking supper. Then he crept out of the wagon, a mass of aches from the tension of keeping himself motionless in the wagon all day. He went into some underbrush with his sack of food, drank water from his flask, and ate some cheese and a tortilla, trying to ignore the scent of the meal the Quinteros were enjoying.

Lewallen's discovery as stowaway came the third day of the journey, when they camped that night on the plains and he started down out of the wagon to fill his flask from the wagon water bucket.

Martin was the one who discovered him. He looked up

from where he was silently greasing the axles of a wagon wheel when Lewallen threw a leg over the back to get down.

"*Lewallen!*" The name was a hiss of astonishment. "You were not to come with us!"

Lewallen pleaded, straddling the top of the wagon bed, "I couldn't wait for you to fetch my sister back to me in Santa Inez, Martin. I want to take Eula Bee away with me just as soon as your pa gets her back from the Indians. Help me, Martin. You promised me that you would back in Santa Inez, remember?"

Martin put his finger to his lips, came up to Lewallen, and whispered, "I remember, but the Comancheros will be very angry that you are here. They might beat you and turn you out alone on the prairie. I do not know what they will do to you. You make me afraid."

"Do you have to tell them that I'm here?" Lewallen asked all at once. It had been a piece of luck to have Martin discover him. "You're my friend, aren't you?"

"*Si*, I am your friend. But what if one of them finds you? What if my father finds out that you are riding in the wagon he drives?"

"I'll worry about that when the time comes, and maybe if we're careful, it won't ever come, Martin."

"But my father and uncles will take the trade goods out of the covered wagon when we get to the valley where the Comanches are to meet us."

"Couldn't you do that, Martin? You could offer to get out the blankets and things they'll want while they do the trading and talking with the Indians."

"Lewallen, the Indians might try to look into the wagon."

"Can't you sit on the seat with a musket and keep them from looking inside? Offer to do that chore, too. I bet that's where your pa and uncles had it in mind for you to be all along while the trading is going on."

Martin's dark eyes were troubled. "I will try. But if the men find you, do not tell them that I knew you were here."

"I promise you that. I won't get you in trouble, too."

"Come down now then. I'll go to the campfire and make some noises so they won't hear you. If I hit a pot with a stick, it will be a warning to you to be careful and get out of sight."

"*Gracias*, Martin."

THIRTEEN

Rendezvous

Lewallen was visited by Martin again and again before they arrived at the Indian meeting place. Each time Martin clambered down into the wagon to fetch something for his uncles and father—who were amused at his sudden eagerness to do so much work—he made a good deal of noise, first calling out something in order to let Lewallen know that he and not one of the others was coming.

He always talked in whispers as he told Lewallen how far they'd come, and each time he brought some smuggled food and water to quench the thirst caused by the terrible heat of July. The very first time Martin climbed down into the wagon, he and Lewallen arranged a system of signals. Martin would whistle a certain fandango dance tune whenever it was safe for Lewallen to get out of the wagon at night. When he heard this tune, Lewallen knew that the Quintero brothers were gathered around their campfire.

The second time Martin came into the covered wagon, Lewallen discussed his plan with him. Its dangers made Martin gasp and stare at Lewallen in admiration, though he was shaking his head at the same time. Yet he didn't go back on the promise he had made in Santa Inez to help him.

And Martin never once said that the promise had been made before he had known that Lewallen planned to go to the rendezvous with the Comancheros.

Still, even with Martin's aid, Lewallen often caught his breath in fright during those last days of travel. Pablo Quintero sat only a few feet from Lewallen, and he had a habit of turning around unexpectedly on the wagon seat to look behind him or to toss his wool serape onto the load of trade goods. Lewallen dared not for an instant sit up in the wagon on top of the trade goods to cool off in the breeze that sometimes mercifully blew through the wagon.

Lewallen could tell one hot night that they had arrived at the valley, because there seemed to be so much unusual excitement among the Comancheros. The men kept calling back and forth to one another as they set up their camp for trading and, by the light of a moon that was nearly full, began to unload the two-wheeled cart that had carried the heaviest trading goods.

From talks with Martin, Lewallen knew that trading whiskey with the Indians called for a special kind of preparation. Early that morning the Comancheros had halted and unloaded the kegs from the cart and put them into their open wagon. Martin and one of his uncles had gone off in the wagon to a gulch a number of miles away from the trading valley. There they would bury the whiskey in the sides of the gulch and keep the hiding place secret until all the rest of the trading was over with and the Comancheros had got the cattle from the Indians. Then Martin Quintero would stay behind alone with the Comanches until his father and uncles had a good start back to New Mexico Territory. When Martin thought they had enough of a lead, he would mount up and lead the Indians to the whiskey. Once they were there and busy with digging out the kegs, Martin would ride hell-bent for leather westward and catch up with the others.

As he'd told Lewallen proudly, "Often a boy Comanchero who is light in weight is the one who does this work. My father did it as a boy, and so did my grandfather before him. It is very risky. The Indians grow dangerous when they are drinking. They will drink some of the whiskey in the gulch, but most of it they will bring back on a travois and pack horses to their camp."

Lewallen had looked aghast at his friend and said, "That's a wicked thing to do, Martin, giving liquor to the Indians. They might get crazy wild drunk and go out scalping and killing."

Martin said, "There are no people settled near this valley. That is why it was chosen. No one comes there but Comanches, Kiowas, and we Comancheros. By the time the Indians leave their camp, they will have drunk all of the whiskey."

Lewallen felt sure that if Small Buffalo showed up this summer at the rendezvous, he'd want to have a share of the Comancheros' whiskey—just as he'd wanted Eula Bee Collier.

At the trading destination, Lewallen dared not come down at night out of the covered wagon because of the Quintero men busying themselves around it. He must stay hidden and wait for Martin to return from the gulch and his chore of burying the whiskey kegs. In the meantime, he prayed that the Quinteros didn't come to the covered wagon and rummage about in it and find him.

He peeked often through the tiny holes in the canvas on each side of the wagon, seeing what little he could through them. He didn't expect to sight the Comanches yet, because Martin had told him that it was their habit to arrive only after the Comancheros' camp was completely ready for trading.

At last Lewallen saw Martin and his uncle drawing up in the open wagon and get down to eat with the other traders. Afterward, as he'd expected, Martin came at once to the covered wagon, whistling the lilting dance tune, and climbed inside. He told Lewallen about burying the whiskey and assured him that he was to unload the lightweight trade goods so he need not worry.

Lewallen whispered to his friend, "Where are the Comanches?"

"They are coming. There are hills all around this valley. I went to the top of one of them with my uncle, who has a spyglass. We looked to the south and saw riders a distance away. There were many of them. My uncle said they are Indians, though they were too far away for me to be sure. The Comanches will set up their camp tonight, and tomorrow we will trade with them."

Lewallen muttered, "I sure hope Small Buffalo is coming here tonight. If he shows up, will you let me know, Martin?"

"I will ask my father to point out the Kiowa to me. If he is here, I will strike the side of this wagon four times with the water dipper. But you must wait until the trading takes place tomorrow for my father to ask the Kiowa about your sister. Tonight the Comancheros and the Comanches smoke pipes together to show that both come in friendship. There will be no trading and no Indians will come before that time, though some of them may visit us tonight."

"Martin, will you hit the wagon five times with the dipper if you happen to see a little girl with red hair anywhere in the camp or if you get word about her?"

"I promise you that I will. I must go now, Lewallen." Grabbing a bolt of yellow calico, Martin scrambled out, leaving Lewallen perched atop some of Cabral's trade blankets, looking at the moon-drenched canvas of the wagon top.

Some hours later the Indians came. From his hiding place Lewallen could hear the familiar noises of a camp being set up. Excitedly the shrill voices of the women called back and forth to one another. Before long he smelled the smoke of their cook fires. Often he could hear the voices of the Comancheros when they were near the covered wagon, and every time he drew in his breath. But, as Martin had promised, no one came down into the wagon.

Who were these Indians—Yellow Wolf's band, one of the seven other Comanche bands, or a combination of bands traveling together?

Kneeling on a pile of blankets, looking out of the peepholes in the canvas, Lewallen at last saw three of the Quintero brothers and Martin walk away together in the direction of the Indian camp. Yes, they were going to smoke now, and when that ceremony was over, Martin had said they'd come back here with some of the more important Indian visitors, who would look at the trade goods by moonlight.

Lewallen Collier waited, biting at his fingers, although he knew that the smoking would be a long-drawn-out business.

He waited and waited and at last heard the one Quintero brother who'd stayed behind with a musket to guard their goods call out a greeting in both Spanish and Comanche.

Lewallen excitedly put his eye to the peephole. The first thing he saw was Pablo Quintero in company with a broad-bodied, middle-aged brave he didn't recognize, though judging by the Indian's two braids he was a Comanche, not a Kiowa. There were other Indians walking behind Pablo and the Comanche. One of them was surely Many Horses, and Lewallen's heart beat faster at the sight of his former master, a man he liked but could not be a son to. The other warriors with the Comancheros and Many Horses were unknown to Lewallen, though none was a Kiowa.

Holding his breath, Lewallen watched Martin saunter over to his wagon and saw him glance briefly upward. Then he heard a rattling noise at the water bucket and knew that Martin was drinking. Afterward came the signal that he had longed for, four little rappings with the dipper, as if Martin was shaking excess water out of it. Yes, Small Buffalo was here! Lewallen waited in a fever of hope for one more rap, but it didn't come. So Martin hadn't spotted Eula Bee or heard anything about her, at least not yet.

Lewallen kept watch until the Indians had inspected the barrels of arrowheads, sacks of tobacco, bolts of cloth, and boxes of knives, pistols, and trinkets. Then they went back to their own camp, and Pablo Quintero set up a series of rotating night watches to guard the trading camp.

The trading would begin with the morning light.

Just before dawn Martin climbed up into the covered wagon to bring out all of the trade goods and set them out on the prairie. After doing so, he came up again and this time brought his own blanket roll and those of his father's and uncles' into the wagon. He said, "Lewallen, now you will still have something to hide yourself under if you must." He went on hastily, "My father says that he plans to ask Small Buffalo about your sister this morning."

Lewallen mumbled, "I sure hope he'll give her up to you."

"If this Kiowa *has* your sister with him, my friend." And Martin clambered out to obey the shouting of one of his uncles.

Later Martin sat with a musket resting on his knees on the seat of the covered wagon, never once looking behind him. Lewallen observed the trading through the peepholes. He watched the Indians, some of whom he recognized as being from Yellow Wolf's band, haul Texas steers on ropes to the Comancheros and barter them for whatever goods struck their fancy. He soon noticed that a large number of the Indians didn't carry off arrowheads, cloth, or pistols but went away empty-handed, and he guessed that they had traded for the hidden whiskey.

Midmorning Many Horses and his second wife, plump Holds the Arrows, came with a steer and went away with tobacco, cloth, and knives. How happy Holds the Arrows looked with the length of scarlet cloth in her arms. She carried it tenderly as if it were an infant.

But where was the Kiowa? Where was Small Buffalo?

At last, around midday, Small Buffalo arrived in all his splendor. He was dazzling in his beaded-and-fringed buckskin as he strolled about with Snow Moon, who walked behind him, hauling on the ropes of two steers her husband meant to trade. Small Buffalo's one long braid below the two crow feathers shone like black silk while the silver ornaments and pearly seashells fastened in it caught the sunlight, twinkling. He was beautiful but deadly, bold, and ambitious. There was no red sash about his waist as yet, although Lewallen was very sure the young warrior still desired it greatly.

Lewallen looked on as Snow Moon gave up one steer for a bolt of blue cloth, a sack of coarse brown sugar, an iron kettle, and a copper pot. She looked poorly, he thought. Her dress was tattered, and her cheeks had been knife gashed not long ago, which told Lewallen that she knew of the cavalry's attack on the Kiowa camp and had cut her face to mourn the death of her husband's people.

Lewallen watched with a mounting feeling of anger while Small Buffalo looked haughtily down his nose at the Comancheros' goods, refusing to barter the second steer for anything the Quinteros offered him. At last the Kiowa turned about to Snow Moon and with a gesture ordered her to give the second steer to one of the traders. Small Buffalo had decided that he wanted whiskey for it. Lewallen nodded from his hiding place. This was something he'd expected, and it didn't interfere with his plan.

At this point Pablo Quintero came striding up with a poke of Lewallen's Fort Belknap beads in each hand. He couldn't hear what the Comanchero said because they were too far away, but he had no need to. As Pablo Quintero spoke to Small Buffalo, he opened a sack of the glass beads the Indian women like to use in decorating clothing and let the bright stream of glass flow into his hand. Lewallen saw how Snow Moon eyed the beads, but they held no interest for her husband. Small Buffalo looked down at them, said something, and walked away from the place where the market was being held. Lewallen anxiously chewed the insides of his cheeks. This reaction could mean one of three things—that the Kiowa didn't have any captive to sell to the Comanchero, that he had no intention of trading any captive for beads, or that he was refusing to ransom his captive for any price. But if Small Buffalo didn't have a captive, would Pablo Quintero bother to approach him with Lewallen's trade goods? Or had Quintero simply been seeking information?

He'd have to wait to find out, wait helplessly as his anger and frustration mounted. Martin would come down into the wagon as quickly as he could, and he'd bring news. Perhaps his father had even caught sight of Eula Bee!

It was late afternoon, the end of the trading day, before Martin could come. Once in the wagon, he told Lewallen, "I asked my father about your sister, Lewallen. The Kiowa says he doesn't have any captives. My uncle Lucho told my father, though, that he saw a girl with red, curling hair in the Indian camp. She may be your sister." Martin hurried on, "Lewallen, the Comancheros are going to break camp now. My father couldn't ransom any captives this time, though he thinks there are captives here with the Comanches. My uncles will start to toss the blankets and cloth the Indians didn't take away with them into this wagon soon. They are in too great a hurry to leave to come down inside and pack them properly."

Lewallen burrowed under the protective bedrolls only seconds before the Quintero men began feverishly throwing trade goods into the wagon from the rear. He had only a moment to wish Martin, who was already climbing out, good luck in the riding he must do now and to tell him, "I am still going to go on with my plan."

Lewallen would stay hidden and be driven away in the wagon until Martin came galloping back to the New Mexico-bound caravan. And that moment, he knew, would be hours from now.

"When he comes, then it'll finally be time for me! Time for me to do something about Eula Bee," Lewallen muttered to himself, as a bolt of calico came hurtling into the wagon, unrolling as it fell, covering him from head to foot with bright-blue cloth.

He didn't dare come up to watch the Comancheros' departure, hoping for a glimpse of Eula Bee, because Pablo Quintero was so close to him on the wagon seat. But he could feel the man's tenseness and eagerness to get away as he cracked his long bull whip over the backs of the mules, urging them to as much speed as possible. The other cart and wagon were surely following closely, and behind them were the stolen Texas cattle, herded along by a Quintero on horseback.

Eula Bee! How Lewallen wished he could bellow her name loud enough for her to hear him. He was sure the Comanchero had seen his sister. There couldn't be another little girl here with red curls. Red hair wasn't that common. It had to be Eula Bee.

The Comancheros didn't make camp that night. They had come to the trading valley by full moon for a reason, so they could travel quickly out of the valley by moonlight and put as many miles between themselves and the Indians as possible.

Lewallen Collier lay in the jolting wagon, waiting. He was waiting and listening for the sound of hooves that meant Martin had overtaken the caravan. Martin had told him that he planned to get away from the gulch before the first Indian had smashed in the top of the first keg. He wasn't even going to get off his horse.

Lewallen had no idea how long he waited, thinking of all the things that had happened to him since his father and brother had ridden off to war. There wasn't much joy to be had from thinking about any of it, except for the months with the Claibornes.

At long last Lewallen's ears caught what they were straining so hard to hear, the swift beating of hooves.

Then came the call in the night from one of the Quintero brothers, "Martin?"

"Quintero!" came the shrill cry in return, followed by a louder drumming of hooves.

Lewallen rose up out of blankets and sat huddled in the darkness. He waited as he listened to Martin tethering Cabral's black horse to the tail of the covered wagon. Was Martin doing that part exactly right? A moment later he saw his friend, only a silhouette in the moonlight, climbing up beside his father onto the seat of the halted wagon.

Pablo Quintero started out again at once. Over the creaking of the wagon wheels, Lewallen could hear Martin's voice boasting to his father of how things had gone at the whiskey gulch and how very fast he had ridden away.

Lewallen listened closely to Martin's words in Spanish.

"Father you were right to tell me I should choose my great-uncle Joseph's swift black horse for tonight's work. The black one is not winded by our ride tonight. I think he could race again tonight, he is so strong."

"There is no cause for you to ride again tonight, Martin. You have done your work and done it well. I feared for you. When he was your age, your grandfather was chased by Comanches. Your great-uncle Joseph was captured as a boy by some Utes he traded with and was their prisoner for a time. His horse fell under him, so they caught him."

"His black horse did not fall with me. He is a good horse."

"Martin, go into the wagon and make a bed for yourself. I will not order a halt to make camp until the moon is as high as it is now tomorrow night. Our mules rested while we traded. They can travel all day tomorrow, too. We must keep on our way."

"*Sí.*"

Lewallen saw Martin scramble over the seat down into the wagon where he pulled a blanket around him, scuffling his boots on the wagon bed, making as much noise as he could to cover the sounds Lewallen made creeping over to him.

When their heads were together, Martin whispered softly into Lewallen's left ear, "All is ready for you. I put the pistol I took with me to the gulch into the saddlebag, and there is a knife as well. There is water in the canteen tied to the saddle. Adios, my friend and good luck to you."

Lewallen found Martin's right hand and squeezed it hard in a good-bye handshake. "*Gracias,*" was his only word, the same word he'd said months before to another Quintero, Mister Cabral. He owed a lot to the Quinteros.

Then he rose up, climbed silently over the rear of the wagon, and moved carefully down over the back into the saddle of Cabral's black. In a few seconds he was able to jerk the loosely knotted reins free, nudge the black in the sides, and start off at a run.

The plot he had hatched with Martin was working—so far it was working!

Martin had told him he would have no trouble finding the right direction to ride. He had only to follow the marks in the prairie grass that the trader's caravan and the animals had made.

FOURTEEN

The Lodge of Small Buffalo

Once he was out of sight of the Comancheros' caravan, Lewallen put the black horse to a steady canter that covered the miles swiftly and easily. As he rode in the moonlight along the wagon tracks, he could feel the strength and striding power of the great animal beneath him. Though Cabral's black had a wicked appearance, he was not at all the evil-natured brute the Colliers had thought. Either that or he'd been very well broken and gentled as a colt by some owner, perhaps Mister Cabral. Deep down Lewallen felt somehow that Cabral would have wanted him to ride the black on his quest for Eula Bee.

He'd hoodwinked the older Quinteros by stowing away in their wagon, and maybe after a time Martin would tell them the true story. But even then the brothers couldn't exactly claim that Lewallen Collier had stolen one of their horses, not when he'd left his stock of trade goods with them, as well as his blue roan.

Martin's wits were very quick. He'd surely think up something to tell his father and uncles about the mysterious rider who'd taken the black horse. He might say that he found an Indian boy from the trading camp hidden down in the wagon and scared him off when he came down inside it. Or perhaps Martin would simply tell the Quinteros the truth right away, that he had helped Lewallen Collier out of friendship and take his punishment for it. He'd point out that Lewallen's roan and beads were still in their hands.

Lewallen had no idea of how many hours he'd been riding when he finally came within sight of the Comanche camp. The tepees would have been visible because of their light color in any event, but tonight there were large fires all about. There also was a fearful din of pistol shots, drumming, loud singing, and what could only be banging of metal on metal. The Indians had brought the whiskey back to their camp and apparently were making short work of it.

He shuddered. Why did the Comancheros have to bring whiskey with them? Wasn't bringing pistols and bullets to the Comanches enough of an evil?

Pistol? The thought made Lewallen recall Martin Quintero's words. He had put his pistol into one of the saddlebags and with it a knife. Reining in the horse, Lewallen reached down, unbuckled the saddlebag, and took up the pistol, which he stuck into his belt. Then beside it he put the knife. Its edge was honed to a razor sharpness.

He gave the black his head, and as the night wind stirred the prairie grass Lewallen rode silently forward. He guided Cabral's horse to the shadowy shelter of some mesquite trees several hundred feet from the camp and dismounted, tethering the horse by his reins to a tree limb. He'd have to walk now. The black horse by his very size would surely attract attention.

His heart beating fast, Lewallen came steathily but swiftly over the grass toward the tepees at the very edge of the camp. How could he tell Small Buffalo's lodge from the others? It had never been painted in any special manner in Yellow Wolf's camp. He would have to go into the camp and search it out—if he could find it at all.

An idea struck him as he passed a travois lying on the ground beside a tepee and saw the shaggy buffalo hide resting on its framework. He took up the hide, wrapped it about him, covering himself from head to foot, and walked past the lodge into the camp, heading for its center. Small Buffalo was an important brave. His lodge, even if unpainted, would be as close to that of the head chief as possible, and the chief's lodge would be painted.

Unnoticed by the Indians, Lewallen Collier, disguised by the buffalo robe, threaded his way in and out among the closely set tepees. He looked carefully at the Indians, but he knew no one by name. As he had thought, this group that came here to trade was made up of people from a number of bands.

Finally Lewallen came across a lodge that was heavily painted, surely the chief's tepee. He began to walk around the lodges next to it, hoping to see something, anything, that would designate one particular tepee as the Kiowa's. He looked for any ponies he might recognize and soon spotted two that belonged to Many Horses, tethered near a tepee. He knew by the ponies and by the symbols painted on the lodge that it belonged to his former master. Pulling the robe down over his face to cover it, Lewallen backed hastily away from that tepee and passed on to others. There was a queer, sick excitement rising in him that grew stronger every moment.

He found the Kiowa's lodge by accident, or by blind luck,

when Snow Moon came out of the entryway of one tepee and went giggling into the lodge directly across from it. A woman's voice called out from the first tepee after Snow Moon. Small Buffalo's wife must have been visiting a woman friend.

This second lodge was the Kiowa's!

Lewallen waited, listening with one ear pressed to the skins of the tepee Snow Moon had gone into, hoping to hear voices over the noises of the camp.

What he heard made him break out into a perspiration. It was the slurred voice of Small Buffalo, then the man's loud laughter at something his wife had said. The Kiowa was inside and not ten feet from him.

Small Buffalo!

Lewallen looked about. There were some Comanche women walking in a group not far from him, but they weren't paying any heed to him. He waited till they had passed.

He hesitated for a time, summoning up his courage. Then, his heart beating hard, he took out Martin Quintero's knife. He walked to the rear of Small Buffalo's tepee, where no one would see him, knelt down, inserted the knife blade at the bottom of one skin, and very quickly slit open the tautly pegged hide. Then he let the buffalo-skin robe fall to the grass. With the knife in his left hand and the loaded pistol in his right, he stepped through the slit into the lodge.

It was lit by moonlight streaming down through the wide smoke hole at its top, and to his relief the prairie moon gave him enough light to see clearly by.

Small Buffalo, who'd been lolling on a heap of skins,

drinking from a gourd, sat up at the sight of the shadowy intruder. He lurched to his feet while Snow Moon backed away on her hands and knees in fright. She was the first to recognize Lewallen.

"Sings His War Song!" came her amazed voice.

Lewallen's gaze swept the tepee for Eula Bee, but he didn't see her.

Finally Small Buffalo found his voice. "*Yee!*" he exclaimed in great surprise, as he stared at Lewallen as if the boy had sprung up out of the earth. All at once the Kiowa threw his arm over his face as if in disbelief, then in one swift motion tossed the contents of the whiskey-filled gourd into Lewallen's face.

As the fiery liquid ran down his face, stinging his eyes, Lewallen said, "My sister. *Ekapi.* Where is she?"

The Kiowa seemed to understand what he wanted because he said in Comanche, "*Kee,*" which meant "no."

The two stood facing each other for a long moment. Then all at once Small Buffalo stooped to pick up Snow Moon's little chopping hatchet set beside the still-smoldering cook fire.

Lewallen didn't wait for him to pick it up. He leaped over the fire and was on top of the Kiowa before he could straighten up. Using all the force he could muster, Lewallen smashed the long barrel of the heavy pistol onto the top of the Kiowa's head, and he fell with a groan onto some rabbit skins.

As the Kiowa sank down, face forward, the rabbit skins heaved up.

Eula Bee Collier rose up out of them to a sitting posture, rubbing her eyes.

At the sight of her Lewallen gasped, then motioned with

the pistol for Snow Moon, who had started to her feet, to stay where she was.

"Eula Bee," Lewallen said softly.

He watched his sister stand up in her beaded buckskin dress, look down at Small Buffalo at her feet, then turn to stare at Lewallen. She spoke no word at all to him. She only stared.

He told her softly, "I'm Lewtie, Eula Bee. I've come to take you home now."

Suddenly Eula Bee jumped out of her rabbit-skin nest. Instead of coming to Lewallen, she fled to Snow Moon and flung her arms around her neck. A torrent of Comanche words came pouring from Eula Bee's mouth.

"*Eula Bee!*" cried Lewallen, who was stunned by her going to the Comanche woman, not to him.

Anger so violent that it poured through him like a boiling river took hold of him. He had tensed his finger on the trigger of the pistol and was ready to fire it into Small Buffalo's body when he became aware of his sister's shrill voice pleading, "*Kee. Kee.*"

He glanced at her and saw how she clung to Snow Moon and the woman to her. Then he looked again at the unconscious Kiowa dandy, Small Buffalo, the cause of so much misery to him. He saw how his one long braid of black hair flung out over a light-colored deerskin. And a thought suddenly struck him!

Lewallen Collier put the pistol back into his belt and transferred the Bowie knife to his right hand. Stooping, he took hold of the Kiowa's greatly cherished braid as close to the man's head as possible, while Eula Bee screamed, and sliced through it, cutting it off.

Next he stuffed it into the front of his shirt. Small Buffalo would be disgraced for the rest of his days. Losing the braid would be worse than being killed by an enemy warrior. There couldn't be any better coup to Lewallen's way of thinking than what he'd just done.

He put the knife beside the pistol, kicked aside the skins between him and his shrieking sister, and jerked her from Snow Moon, who was watching him in silence as a rabbit stares at a rattlesnake about to strike it, paralyzed with terror.

"She's mine. Not yours!" were his only words to her, as Lewallen clapped his hand over his sister's mouth to shut her up and hauled her with him out of the lodge through the slit he'd made in the rear.

Once outside, he picked up the buffalo robe again and pulled it around himself and his kicking, struggling sister.

Eula Bee managed to kick the robe away entirely as Lewallen stepped out in front of the lodge set up to the right of Small Buffalo's. As he fought to get Eula Bee under control again, he saw to his fright and dismay that someone was standing directly in front of him, blocking his way out of the camp. Whoever it might be was wrapped head to foot in a trade blanket, a dark silhouette against the bonfires.

Stepping forward, Lewallen threatened hoarsely, "Get outa my way!"

"Lewallen? Is it you again?" came the quiet, familiar voice, cutting through the camp's noisy din.

"Grass Woman?"

There was a silence from the blanket-wrapped woman while Eula Bee's sharp little teeth chewed on the edge of Lewallen's palm, bringing blood welling through his fingers.

He spoke again, "Grass Woman, I came here to get my sister like I told you I would, and I got a pistol and knife, too."

"Did you kill Small Buffalo, Lewallen? I saw you leave his lodge."

"No, but I sure hit him hard as I could."

Again there was silence, then she said, "You came riding here behind the Comancheros, didn't you?"

"Nope, I came with them. They didn't know I was stowed away in their wagon. Please, Grass Woman, get outa my way."

He had to escape before Snow Moon came out of her trance and ran for help.

She said, "Go now, Lewallen. Many Horses mourns you. I do not want him to know that I spoke with you here tonight. Take your sister away from us if you choose, but you will find she is a Comanche now. Good-bye."

Lewallen hesitated. Was Grass Woman going to give the alarm that he was in the camp? No, it didn't appear that she was if she didn't want Many Horses to know that she'd seen him. Grass Woman was making a present to him of his sister's freedom and his own.

He picked up the heavy buffalo robe and draped it about him again, then started off with Eula Bee, walking bent double, like an old fat Indian woman. He went slowly through the firelit lodges and at last out onto the open prairie with his head down and his eyes on the grass but with his heart pounding inside him like a Comanche drum.

Once he was out of the camp, he flung off the robe, slung Eula Bee up against his shoulder and went at a run for the mesquite and Cabral's horse.

It appeared to him from Eula Bee's struggling that he'd have to tie her up. Well, there was rope enough for that on the saddle, and the cotton cloth around his neck would do for a gag. He hadn't thought she'd fight so hard at being rescued.

"Stop it, Eula Bee. You stop it," he told her, giving her a good shake. When she didn't stop, he told her in Comanche, "*Kee. Keta.*" "No. Don't." She stopped fighting and began to whimper.

"Oh, Eula Bee!" Lewallen mumbled as he pulled off his scarf and tied it across her mouth. She struggled so when he lifted her up into the saddle that he had to tie her hands to its horn. Then he mounted behind her but not before she had kicked him in the face with one foot.

"*Kee. Keta,*" he told her sharply again.

His hopes were fulfilled. His plan had worked, but he surely hadn't expected to have so much trouble from Eula Bee. She was acting more like a bobcat than a little girl.

After he rode out of the mesquite, he took a sighting of the night sky for the pole star. When he had it lined up in the sky, he looked back at the firelit Comanche camp where the noise, if anything, had grown louder. It would be dawn before long, and by that time he had to be out of sight of the camp.

Lewallen headed the black horse southward, in the direction opposite the pole star. Martin had told him that Fort Belknap lay south by east of the trading valley, nigh onto a hundred and sixty miles away from the valley. That was a helluva long distance from where he was right now.

As he rode with his arm about Eula Bee's waist, Lewallen felt suddenly almost giddy with relief. He even laughed aloud. Every time he escaped from Comanche camps he raced away on a black horse. If he could make all those miles to Fort Belknap alive, it would be something to talk about to Captain Claiborne.

The rising sun found Lewallen, as he'd hoped, behind the line of low hills that marked the southern edge of the trading valley. He was on flat prairie ground now, but it was hard country, filled with red-earth chasms that opened unexpectedly in front of a rider. He had to find a way across, down into, and up out of each gully that loomed underneath the black's hooves. He grumbled at the troublesome land, but he was certain that he was traveling south by east. Since he had no landmarks to guide him, he watched the progress of the sun with care and kept it on the proper side of him.

Lewallen halted in the early afternoon and rode into a dense thicket of cat's-claw, beside a drying-up creek, for rest and shelter from the heat. Eula Bee had stopped struggling at dawn and had fallen asleep in the saddle, sagging against his body. She'd awakened midmorning and squirmed, twisted about, but he'd told her, "*Keta,*" again, and she'd stopped. He'd given up trying to speak English to her.

Untieing her, he took her down off the horse, set her on the ground, and removed her gag. He had his first good look at her now. She'd grown taller and was thinner, and her hair was a deeper shade of red. Although her face was tear-streaked and very dirty, it wasn't scarred like Snow Moon's. How queerly she stared at him. Was her expression fear mostly—or was it hate? He seemed to be a pure, dead-rank stranger to her, somebody she was scared of.

198 WAIT FOR ME, WATCH FOR ME

"Eula Bee, don't you know me? I'm Lewtie, your brother," he asked her, as he offered her Martin's canteen to drink from.

Her light-brown eyes searched his face, but he could see no recognition at all in them. She didn't even shake her head to let him know she'd understood what he'd said to her. He sighed, put the canteen to her mouth, and as she opened it poured in water.

Then he left her to take Cabral's horse down to the creek and let him drink. He figured it would be safe enough to take a little time to rest the animal. He caressed the black's neck as he drank, then planned to lead him back and let him graze for a little while. He guessed they could travel easier now.

He knew in his heart that Grass Woman had kept her word not to give the alarm. Snow Moon would, of course, but he was pretty sure she'd attend to her wounded husband first. Even if she started to scream inside the lodge he doubted that anyone would hear her because there was so much screeching and yelling going on in the camp already.

There was something else to think about, too, and he had pondered it a good deal as he'd ridden away from the camp with Eula Bee.

Lewallen doubted that Small Buffalo would tell that the boy who'd once been the slave of Many Horses was the one who'd wounded him and stolen the redheaded child. He wouldn't let Snow Moon tell either. He'd make up some story about an unknown chief, a great warrior of some enemy tribe, who had sneaked into the camp, someone who came by magic and could not be followed. That would make the disgrace of the missing hair a lesser thing —but still a very bad thing!

Well, he was glad he hadn't shot the Kiowa and had that on his conscience.

Standing beside the black horse as he finished drinking, Lewallen reached into his shirt, took out the Kiowa's braid, and looked at it. He shook it once, then dropped it down into the creek. The sluggish current carried it for a few feet downstream, then it disappeared, dragged under the water.

Lewallen went back with the black to where he'd left Eula Bee. As he'd expected, she wasn't there. She had run off. Well, she wouldn't have got far. There wasn't really anyplace for her to go to in the thicket. Quickly he hobbled the black, then set out on foot to find her.

His search was a short one. She'd gone deeper into the briars and was down on her hands and knees glaring at him like a small wild animal. She'd found some berries somewhere and was eating them greedily, stuffing them into her mouth.

"Oh, Eula Bee," he said sadly. Then he got down, crawled in among the thorns, tearing his coat, and dragged her out, scratching and kicking.

He held her off her feet tightly against him, letting her wear herself out with struggling. After a while she began to whine in a high, thin voice, a thing he found worse than fighting. It sounded like a wailing, mourning song the Indian women sang.

He began to sing to cover her eerie sounds. He sang

"Lorena" as he walked back with her to where he'd left the horse. He sang the ballad to its end as Eula Bee had so often begged him to do.

Would she know "Lorena" even if she didn't seem to know him? Maybe so. She'd turned quiet at last. He glanced at her face and saw that she was leaning back in his arms looking directly at him. But there wasn't a flicker of emotion on her face, nothing but a flat stare. Her little freckled face had gone as stony as any face he'd ever seen among the Comanches.

No, apparently she didn't know "Lorena" anymore. Well, he wouldn't sing it to her again. He didn't have the heart to. As far as he was concerned, he wouldn't sing that danged tune ever again!

FIFTEEN
"Sings His War Song"

They rested beside the creek in the thicket until late afternoon. Lewallen struggled to keep his eyes open, but finally he had to sleep in spite of not wanting to. He tied Eula Bee to his waist with a long rope, and for a time, during the hottest part of the July day, they slept.

The boy awoke with a start of fear, hearing rustling sounds about him. His hand went to the pistol set on the ground beside him. No, it wasn't Indians or even Eula Bee, who still slept, but Cabral's big black horse walking about in the thicket. The animal was standing looking down at the two of them as if to say that he thought it was time for them to be off again.

Lewallen got up, awakened Eula Bee, untied her, got the canteen from the saddle, and went with his sister to the creek. There he gently washed her face after filling the canteen again for that night's journey.

It was full dusk by the time they set out. Lewallen felt refreshed by his sleep, though quite hungry. He had picked berries from a bush overhanging the water and had shared them with Eula Bee before they went back to the horse and mounted up. This time Lewallen didn't gag or tie his sister, who seemed not to show any fear of him anymore but not much interest in him either.

"What's the matter with you, Eula Bee?" he asked, as they set off.

There was no answer to his question.

They rode all that night by moonlight, crossing a number of creeks. The black was easy to manage even in deep water. Eula Bee whimpered and flailed her feet as the water flowed waist-deep around her, but Lewallen held her tightly, giving Cabral's horse his head, letting the animal find the safest way to the opposite bank.

Lewallen sighted a grove of cottonwoods near another creek and took the horse into the trees. They'd make their daylight camp here. The sun beat too hot on their heads by day. Though he had a broad-brimmed hat, Eula Bee had none, and he feared she might suffer sunstroke. His hat was far too large for her to wear. When he set it on her head, it came down over her nose, stifling her.

Lewallen's concern was also mounting for the black horse. The animal must not get overtired and must not go lame. Without the horse Lewallen doubted if he and his sister could survive more than two days on foot on the prairie. The horse had to have grass, water, and rest. Lewallen prayed they wouldn't have to outrun wolves or travel miles out of their way to avoid riding through a buffalo herd.

There were no berry bushes at their second camp, but after scouting around Lewallen found some sour fruit on a little tree near the creek and brought it back in his hat for Eula Bee. He was pretty sure as they ate the berries together they weren't poison though they puckered his mouth. Still, they looked familiar to him.

That night traveling, Lewallen walked the black as much as possible to save his strength, while trying to figure out how far they'd come by now. He was thankful that their luck had held and they hadn't heard any wolves, only coyotes, and the only buffalo they'd seen were at a great distance. But how far had they come? A good horse traveling steadily, Lewallen had heard from his pa, could cover fifty or sixty miles a day. While Eula Bee leaned against him, sleeping, Lewallen decided that he wasn't going to make camp again and sleep through the coming day. He'd keep on riding.

He wanted the best possible light so as not miss the east-west wagon road that stretched between Fort Belknap and Camp Cooper, the road he'd seen before. He hoped the growth of new grass this spring hadn't blotted it out so he'd miss it. He had no true hope of hitting the fort dead-center, but the road ran for miles and miles, bisecting the prairie. He had a good chance of spotting it if he kept his eyes open and didn't doze in the saddle.

Riding always with his eyes bent on the grass, Lewallen Collier found the road at last by the rose-gold light of morning. The unused road was fainter than it had been last fall, but there was no mistaking it. Thankfully he reined his horse to the east and set him into a trot that would get them there faster.

"You'll sure take to Mrs. Claiborne," he told his sister, giving her a firm squeeze about her middle.

204 WAIT FOR ME, WATCH FOR ME

Her response dismayed him and made him sigh. A wild kicking followed by a word in Comanche, "*Anaa.*" In English it meant "ouch."

He ransacked his memory for what he'd heard Comanche mothers order their children while riding on the trail from camp to camp. "*Ni-yeh-kar.*" "Sit still and be quiet."

She obeyed at once.

Midmorning Lewallen marked the most welcome sight of Fort Belknap's palisade. Tears of fatigue blinded him for a moment; then he brushed them away and clicked his tongue to the black to quicken his stride. Even if they were all bone-weary and half-starved from travel—the horse, Eula Bee, and himself—he planned to ride into the fort with pride.

The sentry on the catwalk recognized either him or the big black horse and didn't challenge him. Lewallen had expected to enter Forth Belknap by a small side gate, but instead, as he approached, he saw the main gate opening wide for him. A soldier in gray came to stand at attention on each side of it. Through it, inside the fort, Lewallen could spy a small crowd of folks gathered, including the Claibornes. Lord be praised, the captain hadn't been transferred somewhere else yet. He'd worried about taking Eula Bee to strangers.

He felt the shiver that went through her now and tightened his hold on her as he passed the soldiers. "It's all right, Eula Bee. They're on our side."

And then came the cheering, the loud, unexpected cheers saluting Lewallen's success in his quest. They were still

ringing in his ears and making him redden with embarrassment when a soldier came up and grabbed the horse's
bridle as Captain and Mrs. Claiborne came forward out
of the group.

Lewallen spoke to Mrs. Claiborne, "Ma'am, I figured
you were the only person I could bring my sister to. I
hope you don't take unkindly to the idea."

"Oh, Lewallen! How I prayed you would do just that!"

Mrs. Claiborne raised her arms to take Eula Bee as he
lifted his sister out of the saddle. He said, "Ma'am, her
name's really Eula Beatrice, but we call her Eula Bee.
Better watch out for her for a spell. She kicks and bites."
He showed his bitten palm, then added, "She's more
Comanche now than Collier. I was warned that would
happen." .

As Mrs. Claiborne left with a squirming, whining Eula
Bee, Captain Claiborne asked, "That's Cabral's horse, isn't
it? Where's Cabral?"

"He's dead. Killed. It wasn't the Indians who killed him,
but the Yankee troopers from Fort Union. Because I was
his pardner, I got his horse. His two kids are dead too."

"Well, well." Claiborne shook his head. "All right, you
dismount and come to my quarters and eat and sleep.
Then you can tell me your story. I'll bet it's one worth
listening to."

"Yes, sir, I guess maybe it might be." Lewallen reached
into his belt and handed the pistol and knife down to
Captain Claiborne with the words, "Will you keep these
for me, please? I won't be needing them here."

"Were these weapons Cabral's, too?" asked the captain,
as he took them.

"No, sir. They're his family's, though. His folks have his trade goods now."

"Lewallen," the captain asked, "did you ransom your sister?"

"No. I didn't pay out one single bead for her. I took her away with me. But I'll tell you the story later."

"Good Lord, boy!" Claiborne's eyes were filled with wonder as he watched Lewallen dismount.

After a breakfast of fried eggs and bacon and a long sleep in the guest room, Lewallen came to the Claiborne parlor to talk to his hosts. He was feeling like himself again but wondered how and where Eula Bee was.

Mrs. Claiborne was sewing on a piece of green calico, something small that looked suspiciously like a little girl's gown. She held it up for Lewallen to see. She said, "Your sister is still sound asleep in my bed, Lewallen. She let me feed her hominy grits and drank some warm milk I fixed for her, but that was all she'd take before she dropped off. I got her out of her Indian clothes and into an old shirt of my husband's."

"Did Eula Bee talk to you, ma'am? She only talked to me in Comanche."

"No, not one word, Lewallen."

"We shall see what we shall see when the girl wakes up," Captain Claiborne put in. "Now, Lewallen, tell us everything that happened from the moment you rode out of here with Cabral."

Choosing his words with care while Mrs. Claiborne went on sewing, Lewallen told of the visits to the Comanche camp, of Yellow Wolf's lie about Eula Bee, and of the attack by the Yankee troopers from Fort Union on the Kiowa camp.

Lewallen tried to be as just as he could telling them about Cabral. "Mister Cabral wasn't so bad a man as folks thought. He liked to keep to himself a lot and didn't sugar-coat what he said, but he wasn't bad. Even when he was dead, he helped me find my sister."

"How could he do that?" asked Mrs. Claiborne, who by this time was clutching the green dress to her.

Lewallen told of the white stone necklace and of his journey to Santa Fe to Cabral's family. He ended with, "So I joined up with the Comancheros there and learned quite a bit of Spanish from my friend, Martin. I went along with the Comancheros to where they did their trading with the Indians because I figured Small Buffalo might come there with Eula Bee, and he did. I had a plan to get my sister back, and I was lucky that it worked."

Captain Claiborne nodded. "I heard you say that you didn't ransom her with beads but simply took her away with you. How did you do that?"

"Well, sir, the Comancheros went off home with my beads, and I went off alone with Cabral's horse and Martin's pistol and knife back to the Comanche camp. I cut open Small Buffalo's tepee skin and hit him on the head with the pistol handle. He was pretty drunk. Then I thought about shooting him."

"Merciful heavens!" Mrs. Claiborne cried.

"But I didn't shoot him, though some folks would say he deserved it. No, all I did was cut off his hair because Eula Bee was yelling no at me in Comanche. She rattled me plenty. So I took her out of the tepee with me after I cut the braid off, and later I dropped it in a creek somewhere in a thicket."

"Good Lord, you cut off his scalp lock!" Captain Claiborne wiped his forehead with one hand, then pushed his chair back on its rear legs and slapped his knees. He started to laugh, and then he said to his wife, "My dear, that Kiowa won't show his face in his tribe for years and years. Lewallen stole the man's honor. His honor would mean far more to that Indian than his life."

"I don't understand at all," said Mrs. Claiborne.

"I think I do, ma'am," Lewallen told her. "I sort of figured it that way, too. Anyhow it was better than shooting him. What I did would've pleased my ma. So to get on with the story, I started out with Eula Bee fighting me every step of the way, and then I ran into Grass Woman."

"The woman who's a white captive, the one married to Many Horses?" asked the captain.

"Yes. We talked for a bit; then she said good-bye to me. I guess she didn't tell the Indians I came there at all."

"Did you see Many Horses, too?"

"No. I'm glad to say that I didn't. Maybe he wouldn't have let me go the way she did."

Captain Claiborne asked all at once, "What did you think of the Comancheros, Lewallen?"

"They're all right, sir, as a family. I could never have rescued Eula Bee without Martin's help. I don't mind some of the trading they do with the Comanches, but I sure don't take to their trading for pistols and whiskey in return for cattle stolen from Texans. They used to trade just for fur pelts and iron a long time ago, but the Comancheros must've let the Indians know they wanted steers more than furs."

Claiborne nodded. "It's a very bad trade, one that'll have to be stopped when the War's over. So now you know why I kept it quiet around here that Cabral used to be a Comanchero. He'd been pointed out to me in El Paso as a one-time Comanche trader, and I remembered his face from that time. I was afraid that some of my soldiers would put a knife into him if they knew what he used to do."

Lewallen nodded in return. "He sure loved his kids, and he was good to me. I know he would have got Eula Bee back for me somehow, too, if he could have." He let out a sigh starting from the toes of his boots. "She's still a big worry to me, though. The last thing Grass Woman said to me was that Eula Bee was a Comanche now."

"But that isn't true, Lewallen!" came from Mrs. Claiborne.

"Ma'am, she doesn't know who I am, her own brother."

"But, Lewallen, think of what she's been through and how little she still is. She's seen her mother and brother killed and scalped, been a captive for over a year, and kept apart from you on purpose. She's been passed from Yellow Wolf to Small Buffalo. Finally, she's seen the Kiowa attacked and, to her way of thinking, in danger of being shot by you, someone she'd been told she was not to associate with. You say she ran to the Indian woman. I imagine she thought of Snow Moon as the nearest thing to a loving mother she had. Certainly, your sudden appearance in Small Buffalo's lodge, awakening her from sleep without any warning at all, would have been a further shock to her. I think her mind must be affected by all this, Lewallen."

"Yes, ma'am, maybe so. I wish I knew how to help her."

"Well, Lewallen, some wounded minds can heal as well as wounded bodies," came from Captain Claiborne, who'd set his chair down again. "We'll see how the little girl gets along after she's had a good rest with us. Lewallen, we wrote your father about your searching for your sister, but there hasn't been any answer from him. We haven't had any news from the East for months. I wish I knew more about what was happening back there. We're so isolated out here."

"Sir, I got some news of the War from a Yankee I met. Us Confederates won some battles back there last year. Maybe we won some more by now. The Yankees have been winning the scraps in New Mexico Territory, though, and driving us out of there."

"Yes, some riders bound for the East did come through with that bad news last month. We may have lost the War here in the West. Do you want me to write your father again, telling him you found your sister and that you are safe here at the fort?"

"I'd thank you kindly if you would, sir. Tell him I got her back and she's all right, and so am I. You needn't tell him all the things I just told you. It'd only worry him."

Mrs. Claiborne put in, "Lewallen, you could write him soon, yourself. All you have to do is pay close attention to your schoolwork here."

Lewallen winced, then said, "Yes'm."

"I'll be delighted to help you with the spelling," she said, pulling her needle and thread through the gown that was to be Eula Bee's.

A shadow came over Lewallen's face as he gazed at the small dress. When she wore it, his sister would look like her old self again; at least on the outside she'd be Eula Bee Collier again. But on the inside, who was she? A Comanche as Grass Woman had predicted? Was Mrs. Claiborne right? Had Eula Bee's mind been touched and warped by the terrible things she'd seen? She could even have revisited the Kiowa camp, too, after the Yankee troopers and captives had left it. Perhaps Small Buffalo had learned of the massacre and gone back to his band and had brought Eula Bee there with him and Snow Moon again. After all, Snow Moon's face had been gashed in sorrow for a warrior. That would have been a dreadful sight for her to see—for anyone to see, for that matter.

He said quietly, "I hated Small Buffalo but not all of the Indians I got to know. Even if they do hurt their prisoners and make them fight one another, I'm sorry for the Comanches. They live a mighty hard life, harder than a white settler's life. They don't understand us white folks, and we don't think the way they do. We sell them whiskey that turns them crazy. They don't know what whiskey does to a man's head. We know, though, because we've had whiskey for hundreds of years."

"You're right, Lewallen, and in time the Comancheros' ugly trade is going to be wiped out," said Captain Claiborne.

Lewallen spoke sadly, "Martin Quintero's a mighty good friend to me."

"He's young enough to learn another better trade and a less dangerous one."

"That's so, I reckon. I hope he'll be all right till then."

A sergeant's wife gave Mrs. Claiborne a tattered old rag doll that her own little girl had discarded, and Mrs. Claiborne gave it to Eula Bee. Lewallen saw that his sister took it, though that meant little, for Comanche children played with dolls, too. He saw that Eula Bee carried the toy around with her, holding the doll by one leg, letting it trail on the ground, just the way she used to at home. This little thing somehow comforted him.

She didn't speak to him or to anyone else. She wouldn't sit on a stool or chair but mostly squatted, though at times she'd sit on pillows piled on the floor. Before she'd been captured, she'd used a spoon and fork fairly well, but now she scorned them, using her fingers to take food off her plate. When it came to grits or soups, Mrs. Claiborne had to feed her with a long spoon and wipe her face afterward with a napkin. Eula Bee played dolls with the only other little girl her age at the fort, but Lewallen noticed that Eula Bee spoke to her in Comanche, not English.

"What are we going to do about her?" he asked Mrs. Claiborne on the Saturday morning at the end of their second week at the fort.

"Be patient. Wait. Keep an eye on her and wait, Lewallen."

"Wait. Watch her," he'd muttered glumly. "I heard them words before, and they've sure been on my mind ever since." He stalked off to the stables to groom Cabral's horse, which sometimes took his mind off Eula Bee.

Weeks passed slowly. August melted away into September, and there was still no change in his sister as far as Lewallen could see. He felt so downhearted about her that he was even glad to get back to his school lessons to occupy his mind with something other than Eula Bee.

Then, mid-September, news of the War came from the East by a dispatch rider, though there was no letter as yet from Lewallen's pa. The news the rider brought to Captain Claiborne delighted the Texans in the fort. The Confederates had won a second victory in Virginia at Bull Run, and perhaps would soon capture Washington, D.C., and end the War.

That night the Claibornes gave a party in their quarters to celebrate the good news. Lewallen and some soldiers helped clear the parlor of rugs and furniture so there could be dancing. In spite of Eula Bee's constantly queer behavior, Lewallen's spirits brightened as the day went on. Pa and Johnny would be coming home soon when Washington was captured. Then Pa would make a home for all of them somewhere. Pa could maybe make Eula Bee remember him. Or perhaps she might remember Johnny. He was a favorite of hers.

Eula Bee came to the party that evening and sat on some pillows stacked up in a corner. She held her doll tightly and watched the goings on with interest. Mrs. Claiborne had put white silk ribbons in Eula Bee's hair tonight, and her little freckled face shone with cleanliness as she watched the couples waltzing to the music Mrs.

Claiborne played on her cottage organ. Around and around the grown-ups circled, waltzing while Lewallen leaned against a wall, mostly watching his sister.

At last Captain Claiborne called a halt to the dancing and offered a toast to the Confederate victory. When everyone had drunk to the second battle of Bull Run, he announced, "Let's sing the 'Bonnie Blue Flag' now."

Still standing, the guests and Captain Claiborne, except for Mrs. Claiborne at the organ, sang the song that was the new anthem of the Confederacy, one Lewallen hadn't heard yet. He thought it was a stirring tune with all its loud hurrahs.

Afterward there was quiet for a moment. Then Mrs. Claiborne said, "Well, that was very fine. Now let's sing some of the other songs. I' m sure you must be weary from dancing so much."

She lifted her hands off the keyboard, then let them fall, starting the first notes of "Lorena," wrenching Lewallen's heart.

Most of the other people seemed to know the words and sang the popular ballad along to the music, but not Lewallen. He hung his head in silence, lost in the unhappy memories that went along with it. As he listened to the off-key baritone efforts of the soldier who was leaning next to him, he longed for the ballad to be over with.

All at once as the song neared its end, he felt the soldier nudging him as if to urge him to finish "Lorena" with him. The man meant well. He couldn't know how he felt about that song.

Lewallen moved away from him and muttered, "I don't want to. I don't like that tune."

Again there was the annoying nudge and then the soft words, "Look at the little gal. Look at your sister, boy!" Lewallen's head jerked up, and he stared across the parlor at Eula Bee, who'd been sitting down. She'd got to her feet and walked to the center of the parlor. There she stood, a little lonely figure, behind the guests clustered about the cottage organ.

As the last words of "Lorena" trailed off, Eula Bee lifted her arm, pointed at Lewallen, and said something in Comanche. Then, frowning at him, she stamped her foot and repeated what she had said. Everyone turned to stare down at her in an interested curious silence, but she looked only at Lewallen.

"What did she just say to you, Lewallen?" Captain Claiborne asked him.

"She said my name, the one the Indians gave me. She called me 'Sings His War Song.'"

Mrs. Claiborne spun around on the organ bench, her peach-colored taffeta skirts whirling, and demanded, "What was that you said just now, Lewallen?"

Painfully aware that everybody was staring at him, Lewallen mumbled, "I said she called me 'Sings His War Song.' That's what the Comanches named me because I sang so much to Eula Bee when I was in their camp. I kept on singing her favorite song over and over again."

"Singing? What song did you sing to her?" asked Mrs. Claiborne.

"It was 'Lorena,' the tune you just played. She doesn't pay any heed to it anymore, though. I sang it to her on the way here, but she didn't remember it, even though it used to be her favorite."

Mrs. Claiborne looked from him to Eula Bee, and then she said, "Lewallen, sing 'Lorena' now! Right this very minute. Everybody else please keep quiet so we can hear only Lewallen's voice. Sing it while I accompany you on the organ, Lewallen."

So, while Mrs. Claiborne softly played "Lorena," Lewallen, red with embarrassment, sang it aloud, keeping his eyes fixed on Eula Bee. Singing it made him melancholy because of all the things it made him remember. Lewallen closed his eyes in the middle so no one could see the tears coming to his eyes.

> *"The story of the past, Lorena*
> *Alas, I care not to repeat*
> *The hopes that could not last, Lorena*
> *They live, but only live to cheat."*

Then he felt a touch at his side and a cool, small hand slip gently into his.

"Lewtie?" came the one soft word.

Author's Note

West Texas was, in fact, left almost unprotected during the Civil War. The few military forts that existed were severely undermanned, and many settlers had to fort up for protection from Indians at these military installations or in stockaded farms.

The Comanche Indians, the most powerful and feared of the Great Plains tribes, raided the defenseless Texans' farms with greater fury than ever once the men left for the War in the East. The Comanches and their Kiowa allies killed, pillaged, burned homesteads, and often carried off cattle and children. The cattle were bartered to traders for goods, and the captive children sometimes were bought back by their families. Often, however, these children, who were slaves, eventually became members of Comanche and Kiowa families.

In this novel Lewallen Collier gains the trust of a Comanche and is set out to guard the warrior's ponies. Historical accounts of escaped white captives often include incidents about boy horse herders who ran off on a stolen pony.

The Comanches and Kiowas lived the sort of tribal lives

depicted in this book. The work of the women was hard and had little glory to it, but old time Texans remarked over and over on the ferocity and loyalty of the Indian women. The preferred food of the Plains Indians was buffalo. The buffalo hunt Lewallen experiences is described as it would have taken place among the Comanches. Many Horses' scorning of long-range weapons, such as bows and arrows as well as a pistol on the hunt, is in keeping with the character of a noble warrior.

Small Buffalo would not have been an unusual young brave. The Red Sash existed and was the goal of many Kiowa warriors, though only ten men were permitted to be members. The Kiowas often visited and lived with the Comanches, although they spoke another language. Kiowa men wore a different, very special hair style, the chief feature being one very long braid of hair. Hair was vital to the psychology of the Indian male in many tribes. The practice of scalping enemies had a religious significance. Lewallen's cutting of Small Buffalo's braid would have had a meaning and importance to the Kiowas that would be difficult to comprehend today. It was true vengeance.

What I've written about clothing, food, travel, hunting, language, trail camps, and winter camps is accurate and drawn from a number of sources, such as: *Comanches, the Destruction of a People* by T. R. Fehrenbach; *The White Chief* by George P. Belden; *The Comanches, Lords of the South Plains* by Ernest Wallace and E. Adamson Hoebel; *Comanche Texts* by Elliott Canonge; *The Indians of Texas* by W. W. Newcomb, Jr.; *Comanche Land* by Emmor Harston; *The Plains Indians and New Mexico* by Alfred B. Thomas; *Comanche Days* by Albert S. Gilles, Sr., *The*

Kiowas by Mildred P. Mayhall; and *Saynday's People, the Kiowa Indians and the Stories They Told* by Alice Marriott.

For actual accounts of the lives of captives among the Comanches I've used chiefly *The Last Captive*, by Herman Lehman, who lived among both the Apaches and the Comanches.

Life among the Comanches was to our modern way of thinking extremely brutal, with pain, hunger, cold, and death constant companions. Warfare and raiding were the ways in which a warrior gained prominence and wealth in ponies and power. A Comanche brave did not expect to grow old. He expected to die gloriously in battle. Old men were not revered among The People (the actual Comanche name for themelves) for their wisdom and experience. They were thought chiefly useless and were recipients of charity from younger braves. Suicide was common among the old men who could no longer fight and hunt.

The Comanches valued youth and strength and did indeed covet children to keep their bands powerful. They not only raised captives as Comanches, they bought children of poorer, less-powerful tribes to raise as Comanches. The bonds of affection between Comanche foster parents and captive children make a touching footnote to history and often a tragic one.

It's true that the Comanches tortured captives, but many Indian tribes had observed this ugly practice for centuries in their wars against enemy tribes. White captives were not singled out for torturing. This custom was common among warfaring Indian nations long before the Americans pushed westward or the Spaniards came up from Mexico.

Many readers may not have heard of the Comancheros,

the Indian traders from New Mexico Territory. Theirs was a trade dating back to the late eighteenth century and originally was conducted by the barter of pelts for iron from which arrowheads could be fashioned, blankets, cloth, trinkets, etc. It had expanded by 1861 into a trade that focused on pistols, bullets, ready-made arrowheads, and cheap whiskey in exchange for stolen Texas cattle. It is lamentable but true that many Indians found the white man's whiskey very desirable. The Indian had not known of alcohol and its properties before the white man introduced him to it. Many were not able to cope with it and could not understand how the white man managed it.

The trade was carried on by New Mexicans who came annually by cart and pack burro to a special valley in North Texas to meet the Comanches. The valley was known to the New Mexicans as the Valley of Tears because many captives were traded there.

The Comanche-Comanchero trade flourished throughout the disruptive Civil War period and even afterward. It came to an end around 1880 when the Army set out to control the Indians and get them onto reservations. Armed Texas civilians also retrieved their cattle and "dealt with" Comancheros wherever they ran across them. (One old Comanchero was persuaded by torture to reveal the location of a Comanche camp, which the Army later attacked.)

In this story, I've depicted a surprise attack by Yankee cavalry, alerted by their Indian scouts, on a Kiowa camp. It could easily have taken place just as I've written and the two Cabrals killed in the gunfire aimed at Indian males. Indian women and children were led away by soldiers after such raids and held in stockades at forts, then settled on reservations.

Palo Duro County is fictional as is Santa Inez, but Fort Belknap and Fort Union are real frontier forts. I've described them as they were in the early 1860s using *Old Forts of the Southwest* by Herbert M. Hart; *The Dark Corner of the Confederacy, Accounts of Civil War Texas as Told by Contemporaries*, edited by B. P. Galloway; *Texas in the Confederacy* by Colonel Harry McCorry Henderson; and *Five Years a Dragoon* by Percival G. Lowe.

On a much lighter side, readers might be interested to know that the theme song I use for Lewallen and Eula Bee Collier, "Lorena," is a song of the Civil War era. It was composed in 1857 and was a great favorite among Southerners but is not a song associated with the Yankee Army. The words I have used were drawn from the actual ballad, which relates a melancholy love affair.

As usual in writing of the Civil War I've enlisted the aid of Texas-born historian Professor Hal Bridges of the University of California, Riverside. He deserves my thanks for his courtesy and willingness to answer questions for me and for suggesting resource materials.

Patricia Beatty
November 1977